96

Edited by Diane Schoemperlen

COMING ATTRACTIONS
96

This book was written and published with the assistance of the Canada Council, the Ontario Arts Council and others. The editor wishes to thank Andris Taskans of *Prairie Fire*, Joan Harcourt of *Queen's Quarterly*, Kim Jernigan of *The New Quarterly*, Derk Wynand of *The Malahat Review* and Don McKay of *The Fiddlehead* for their generous help.

Acknowledgements: "Drought" by Lewis DeSoto first appeared in *Prairie Fire* and "Zoe in Marais" by Lewis DeSoto was originally published in *Quarry*. "Everett and Evalyne" by Murray Logan is forthcoming in *The Fiddlehead* and "Oh, Henry" by Murray Logan will appear in *The New Quarterly*. "A La Playa" by Kelley Aitken is forthcoming in *Prism International* and "Orchids" by Kelley Aitken was first published in *Grain*.

ISBN 0 7780 1042 2 (hardcover)
ISBN 0 7780 1043 0 (softcover)

Cover art by Lucian Freud
Book design by Michael Macklem

Printed in Canada

PUBLISHED IN CANADA BY OBERON PRESS

Introduction

It is common practice for writers to be identified by their countries: we have Canadian writers, American writers, French writers, Australian writers, British writers, German writers...the list is very long. Every country in the world lays claim to its own. These territorial labels may be a handy way of putting writers in their places (so to speak!) but they fail to convey one of the essential attributes of the imagination: that is, its internationalism. The imagination in general, and the literary imagination in particular, knows no borders and is not limited by geography. The three writers whose short stories are gathered here are all Canadian but acknowledging this hardly begins to identify their work. Their imaginations are well-travelled citizens of the world.

Lewis DeSoto was born in South Africa and writes of his homeland with power and quiet passion. These are understated stories, effective and potent. DeSoto, who now lives in Toronto, studied art at the University of British Columbia and the visual imagery in his work is very strong: each story closes with a resonant image that lingers in the reader's mind long after the reading is done. DeSoto's fiction has appeared in *Quarry*, *Prairie Fire* and *Event*, and has been nominated for a Western Magazine Award.

Murray Logan lives in Vancouver and he does write about Canada. His finely crafted stories of North American life seem familiar enough at first but, as each story begins to unfold, it soon swerves gently off to another territory altogether. Logan has completed an MFA in Creative Writing at the University of British Columbia where he worked with Linda Svendsen and Keith Maillard and was editor of *Prism International*. He has also worked for CBC-TV Western Drama Development and was a winner of the DuMaurier One-Act Play Competition in 1994. A collection of his short fiction will be published in 1997.

Kelley Aitken is a writer, artist and illustrator who lives in Toronto and travels frequently to Ecuador. It is of South America that she writes in these three stories. They are rich with evocative details from another culture, with a sense of dislocation not without humour, and with questions concerning love and loss that might well preoccupy anyone anywhere. Aitken's fiction has been published in *RFR: Resources for Feminist Research, Room of One's Own, Blood & Aphorisms, The Toronto Star, subTERRAIN* and *Grain.*

What these three writers clearly share, beyond their designation as Canadian writers, is a clarity of vision, a precision of language and a great deal of talent.

DIANE SCHOEMPERLEN

Contributions for *Coming Attractions* 97, published or unpublished, should be sent directly to Oberon Press at 400–350 Sparks Street, Ottawa, Ontario, K1R 7S8 before 31 October, 1996. All manuscripts should be accompanied by a stamped, self-addressed envelope.

LEWIS DESOTO

Drought

An airplane passes overhead, making a wide slow arc as it drones into the distance. Someone is going somewhere. From up there the earth might look like a quilt of ochres and browns, broken by the patches of black, still wispy with smoke from the fires the soldiers have left. Scorched browns and burnt yellows baking in the furnace of late summer. Except for one perfect rectangle of blue.

Cerulean, cobalt, ultramarine, turquoise. This blue is sky-blue, azure. A small rectangle of the sky that has been scissored out and let fall to the dry earth on a blazing day in a season of drought.

Here is a swimming-pool of blue water on the parched African plain. A white house, a blue pool and a high protective wire fence. The water is an impossible colour in this dry country. It is a blue that quenches thirst, that refreshes the eyes, that caresses the skin and washes the dust away with a coolness that can hardly be imagined, it is buried so deep in memory.

A heavy wire fence encloses the pool. On the wire a small manufacturer's plaque announces that the fence was fabricated by Kruger Maartens Inc., Johannesburg. Specialists in Security. Along the top of the fence an ingenious arrangement of razor-sharp barbs is guaranteed to deter any intruder.

Behind the fence is the sky-blue swimming-pool, edged with terracotta flagstones. There is a white house beyond the pool, a modern house with featureless white walls and a flat roof. In the big windows the blinds are lowered against the sun.

Along the base of the fence a border of green shrubbery has been planted inside the wire; plants with long spiky fronds and others that have succulent, lozenge-shaped leaves, deep green with contained moisture.

The bright aquamarine water is as still and flat as a picture.

No breeze ripples the surface. The sides and floor of the pool are painted blue and the depth of the water is impossible to determine. It might only be a foot or two, but it also might go on forever, like the sky.

The white buildings dazzle in the sun. A woman comes out of a glass door in the house and walks to the edge of the pool where she kicks off a pair of sandals, stands naked a moment in the light, then dives into the water.

The silence erupts like a sudden exhalation of breath. Water bursts through the air in a spray of stars around her and subsides to the terracotta flagstones with a pattering rain. High overhead two military aircraft boom and flash toward the border.

On the other side of the wire, hidden by the shrubs, a youth squats with his fingers laced though the metal of the fence and watches the bather. The remnants of moisture splashed in the air by her dive reach him as the traces of a fine mist. He puts his lips on the hot steel, tasting what has already evaporated at the first contact with the heated metal. Overhead the airplane has circled back and the rumble of its engines hums through the wire under his fingers.

Reaching through the fence he breaks a bud from one of the plants and places it on his tongue. When his teeth bite through the green lozenge, a bitter, aloe-flavoured liquid squirts into his throat.

The woman surfaces and exhales a sigh, tossing back her head, droplets flashing in a halo around her cropped blonde hair. The waves undulate to the sides of the pool, circles of ripples gradually subsiding until the surface of the water is flat and immaculate again.

Heat.

Silence.

Only her head and shoulders are visible as she holds her face up to the sun, eyes closed. Under her chin the water dances a pale, aqueous reflection. The clatter of distant helicopters approaches across the quiet and the skin of the water shivers with the vibrations.

Now she begins to swim down the length of the pool, feet kicking rhythmically, frothing up a white foam that swirls around the pink soles of her feet. The sound reminds the youth of the stream that used to gush from the reservoir pipes before the soldiers destroyed the dam and put chemicals in the river.

He presses his face against the wire, leaning all his weight against the unyielding metal, watching the liberty of her smooth glide through the water. If he shifts his head in tandem with her motion, she remains contained in the diamond-shaped gaps formed by the wire of the steel fencing. Aquamarine framed by silver. Across the pupils of his eyes a faint sheen of moisture reflects two small, shimmering rectangles of blue.

The sun blazes through the worn cotton on his back and he is aware of the rank odour rising from his unwashed body, mixing with the burnt smell of his clothes. The muscles in his calves ache from the strain of his confined posture but he is afraid to move. In the white house a dog barks briefly until a hard voice silences it.

At the far end of the pool the woman descends below the surface, turning, and for a moment the water is uninhabited, flawless, like a sea, except for the tatters of a wake on the swell. Now she comes up in a slow roll, breathes and turns. As each arm rises, tiny droplets flicker through the air like silvery pearls, fracturing the sunlight as they break.

When she reaches the near side of the pool she rests, standing with her back to him, elbows leaning on the edge. She is so close now that her image is captured in the net-like pattern of the shadows cast by the fence. He can hear the quick, shallow gasps of her breathing as it eases into sighs.

Her skin is the colour of an almond shell, lightly tanned by the sun, beaded with moisture. His own hand gripping the wire next to her image is brown, the nails cracked and blackened with soot and ashes. She turns slightly to her left and shakes her hair again, scattering pearls. Her naked breast is visible, absolutely round, like a fruit. He moves his finger slightly and it seems to stroke across the moisture on the wet skin.

He watches a droplet of water trickle from the pale blue light under her chin and move down over her chest, curving across the slope of her breast to the nipple, sparkling as the sun refracts through the liquid. Beneath his ragged shirt a dribble of warm sweat seeps from his armpit and down his ribs. Reaching carefully for another green bud from the bushes, he places it on his tongue. The woman begins to swim again, faster this time, churning up the water, sending a wash heaving over the sides of the pool as she submerges at the far end and turns to come back. Water is splashing everywhere, flung into the air like a curtain of rain by her wheeling arms and legs. It flows onto the terracotta walk and streams across the stones.

His throat is dry, parched with thirst, and his skin feels like the broken clay at the bottom of a cracked riverbed. Yet he can taste the water she moves through, feel it sliding blue over his skin and across his lips in cool cerulean waves as it pours into his mouth, filling him to bursting. He is submerged in the blue pool, drinking of the water behind the fence. His insides become stretched to the breaking point by an overflow of the swirling liquid until his stomach brims over and his distended bladder aches for release.

He fumbles with the buttons of his shorts as he crouches, and releases his penis, letting a hot stream of urine burst against the fence and splash over the shrubs. He shuts his eyes against the glare and allows a cool, dark wave of relief to wash over him.

When he opens his eyes the woman is pulling herself from the pool a few feet away. He freezes in position, like an animal, one soiled hand fixed on the fence, the other still grasping his penis.

She is standing on the flagstones now, breathing hard from her exertions and gazing through the fence into the dry distance. A sound like thunder comes across the arid landscape, followed by the flat clatter of machine-gun fire. On the horizon a plume of mustard-coloured smoke drifts into the air. An airplane rises in ascending circles.

The water streams down her body and collects in puddles at her feet, staining the terracotta a deep reddish brown around her painted toenails. She shakes her head and runs her fingers through her hair and a pattern of drops traces across the walk, evaporating in little puffs of steam as soon as they touch the hot stone.

The juncture of her thighs is at his eye level, the secret declivities of her body clearly visible through the triangle of wheat-coloured hair.

Tiny droplets of golden water clinging to the hairs shimmer in the light. A faint scent drifts from her skin as it dries in the sun. Between his fingers he feels the sudden firm pressure of his own flesh as it swells and rises.

She puts a foot into her sandal and reaches down for her towel. At that precise moment, as she stoops, her eyes meet his. They see each other. Then with a small yelp of surprise she steps back and stares down at him, half raising a towel in front of her. Her eyes move lower and see his unbuttoned shorts. An expression of disgust crosses her face.

"What the hell are you doing?" she shouts.

He scrambles to his feet, fumbling to close up his shorts.

"Get away from here! You ugly monkey, you dirty thing!" The metal of her cries is breaking the air.

Words rises to his lips and become ashes. His tongue is a stone. He turns and runs back across the charred field, his vision clouded by shame and anger. Other voices are raised in alarm over the sound of the woman's shouts. The dogs are barking. He runs harder. Where his bare heels strike the ground little puffs of ash rise from the blackened soil. Above the village thunder is filling the sky with yellow smoke.

Zoe In Marais

Eleven months after her father died Zoe ran away from home. She was fifteen. Soon after dawn, with her one small suitcase, she walked up the hill from the farm, her new shoes dangling by their straps from her free hand, the sand of the road soft against the soles of her bare feet.

Beside the road the fields were silent in the early morning light except for an ungainly black bird with a long tail, flapping just above the dry grasses.

When she reached the top of the hill and the paved road Zoe sat down on a boulder and brushed the grains of sand from her feet before putting on her white socks and shiny black shoes. A little farther along at the solitary yellow post that marked the bus-stop she set her suitcase down and turned to face the east where the sun was a sliver of red edging over the horizon.

In the valley at the bottom of the hill her mother and step-father would sleep for another two hours before the sun touched the walls of the shaded farmhouse.

At the Joubert Street terminal Zoe left the bus and with her suitcase in hand she walked out into the city. Shabbily dressed men stood in idle groups in the patches of sunlight on the street corners or lay asleep along the grassy verge that ran down the centre of the boulevard. The jacaranda trees were pink with blossoms, fragrant in the morning air, growing in a long line down one side of the boulevard. There was little traffic.

Zoe did not like the way the men looked at her and after a few uneasy blocks she returned to the bus terminal and found a bench near the ticket office, where she tucked her suitcase close between her feet.

From her vinyl purse she took an address book, the pages mostly bare, and leafed through the few entries; girls at school, the radio station in Lourenco Marques where she sent requests for pop songs, the name of a pen pal in Texas with whom she had exchanged only one letter.

An old postcard slipped from between the back pages and fell to her lap. It was from her friend Bella who had moved away to the town of Marais more than a year ago. Bella and she were not close friends, it was only because they were rural neighbours and rode the same bus to school that they had met at all. Bella had come to visit at the farm on two occasions but she had never invited Zoe to her own home.

One day during the autumn term Bella was not there when Zoe boarded the bus and she did not see Bella again. It was not until she received the postcard some months later that Zoe discovered her friend had moved away to another town.

She turned the card over in her hands and studied the picture on the other side, where the green and black heights of the Drakensberg mountains were outlined against a sky of puffy white clouds.

Slipping the card back into her address book she went across to the ticket office and asked the man behind the wicket if there was a bus to Marais. The closest stop was Nyslstad, he said, which was fifteen miles from Marais. With one of the crisp banknotes she had taken from her stepfather's wallet that morning Zoe bought a ticket then went to wait outside.

They arrived in Nylstad just after noon. Zoe got down and squinted at the unfamiliar landscape as the bus drove away into the glare. From a fruit stand she bought an orange and sat astride her suitcase on the gravel at the side of the road. The fruit was sweet and juicy, leaving her mouth and fingers coated with a sticky residue. Then she picked up her suitcase and began to walk.

The long road that stretched out before her shimmered and moved in the heat, pools of water seeming to hover in the distance, always receding as she advanced. They were mirages, she knew. Mr. Potgeiter had explained it in science class and said it was an illusion, light reflecting in a haze off the road's surface, but they seemed real pools anyway and made her long for a drink of water.

In the shade of a thorn tree she paused and removed her cardigan, folding it neatly into her suitcase. The air was cooler on her bare arms when she resumed walking. A truck loaded with bales of barbed wire passed her, and she raised her arm in a wave to the glimpsed driver, then stood listening to the sound of the engine as it faded into the dry silence.

The air was so still that she could hear a humming from the telephone wires on the poles above the highway; conversations endlessly receding across the hot plain where the fields were a dry ochre colour broken only by the ragged black silhouette of a thorn tree in the glare. When she put her hands to the hair at her temples her fingers came away damp with perspiration.

The road seemed endless and her shoes pinched her feet, the hot sensation of a blister like a flame at her heel. She sat down on her suitcase and loosened the shoe buckles a notch and wiped away as best she could the film of dust covering the shiny leather. Behind her in the grass the cicadas buzzed with a steady insect drone.

In the far distance a blur appeared on the horizon where the road shimmered and merged with the sky. It became a vague shape that held for a moment then broke to merge again with the haze. By slow degrees it neared and Zoe was at last able to make out a figure on a bicycle. She got up and went to stand at the side of the road.

The cyclist drew nearer and Zoe saw that it was a black man, pedalling hard with his head down, dressed only in a pair of faded trousers. He did not look up as he passed her with the soft whirring sound of rubber on tarmac and she only had a glimpse of his face, clenched with effort, his features slick with sweat. She watched his bent back and pumping legs until his shape was once more a mere smudge in the distance.

A few minutes later a grey van came down the road from the same direction, traveling very fast. Zoe saw the khaki uniforms of two white policemen in the front as the vehicle whipped by with a crackle of static, the long radio antenna on the roof bent almost double. A hot gust of gasoline fumes blew her hair across her eyes. She picked up her suitcase and began to walk once more.

Sometime later there was the sound of a car approaching but Zoe did not turn around. It slowed as it passed her, a small blue Austin, then came to a gradual stop a few yards farther on. As Zoe came abreast, the window on the passenger side was rolled down and the weather-beaten faces of two elderly women peered at her.

"What are you doing out here, girl? Don't you know there's trouble?"

Zoe shook her head. "I have to get to Marais."

The driver leaned across and looked Zoe over with care. "Are you all alone?"

"Yes. There isn't a bus today."

The woman's eyes moved past Zoe and examined the fields behind her. "All right," she said at last. "You had better get in." She leaned over and unlocked the rear door. "We can give you a lift to Marais."

"Thank you." Zoe pushed her suitcase onto the floor and slid across the seat, feeling the hot leather on the backs of her thighs through the material of her dress. She inched her window down and looked up to meet the eyes of the driver in the rearview mirror.

"Do you live in Marais?" the woman asked.

"No. I'm going to visit my brother. He lives there."

"Couldn't he at least come and pick you up?" The woman's tone was sympathetic but her eyes were watchful.

"He was going to, but his car broke down this morning." The lie sounded entirely plausible to Zoe, and it was almost as if she did have a brother in Marais, who at this very moment was bent over the engine of a battered car with a cigarette dangling from his mouth as he struggled with the motor, aware that Zoe was somewhere out there waiting for him on the long hot road.

The woman pressed her lips together and moved her eyes

back to the road.

They passed a sign with the word "Teahouse" painted on it and ahead a cluster of buildings appeared, the tin roofs glinting silver in the sun. The woman in the passenger seat turned to her companion and in a low voice said, "Do you think it would be all right to stop for a cup of tea?"

"It should be safe out here," the driver answered, slowing the car as she bent forward to study the buildings.

They drove in next to a low farmhouse with plaster walls and a corrugated tin roof. From behind the house an unseen dog began to bark excitedly.

The interior of the teahouse was cool and shadowy and they sat down near the door, ordering tea from a thin woman with a tired face. There were no other customers.

When the tea came Zoe opened her purse to reach for some coins but the driver put her hand over Zoe's and shook her head, counting out the money herself.

Zoe drank the hot, sweet tea in gulps, then sat and looked through the dusty window at the nearby mountains.

The two women sipped from their cups in a silence broken only by the dull clink of the china. Outside, a vehicle pulled up and a door slammed but nobody came in.

After the shade of the tearoom the glare outside was momentarily blinding. Zoe paused for a moment at the top of the steps while her eyes adjusted to the light. Next to the car was a grey police van like the one that had passed her earlier, its rear doors wide open and the motor running. The radio crackled with static.

The women moved quickly to their car, and as Zoe followed, two policemen appeared round the side of the house. Between them they supported the cyclist, his hands manacled behind his back, his body limp in their grasp as his feet dragged in the dust. A dark splash of blood stained the front of his trousers.

As the policemen lifted him to the doors of the van he came to life in a brief struggle of resistance, pulling away from the dark interior of the vehicle. One of the policemen slapped him hard on the side of the head with a flat, ugly sound that made Zoe flinch. The man collapsed into the van and the policeman lifted the dangling legs and shoved them into the vehicle before slamming the doors shut. Behind the building the unseen dog was barking furiously with high, frantic yelps.

"Hurry up!" one of the women hissed at Zoe from the car. She got in and they sped out to the main road, the rear wheels sending up a spray of sand and gravel. Zoe turned and saw the man's bicycle in the dust at the foot of the steps. She hoped that somebody would remember it was there.

Within fifteen minutes they were on the outskirts of Marais and the driver finally allowed her speed to slacken as they entered the small town at the foot of the mountains.

"Where is your brother's house, girl?" the driver asked, watching Zoe again in the mirror.

"He lives just up here." Zoe pointed at random to the tree-lined street on her right. The car drove slowly past the houses. "This one, here." She indicated a small house with an apricot tree in the front garden.

"Thank you very much for the lift, and for the cup of tea," Zoe said, lifting her suitcase from the floor. They nodded curtly to her and watched as she went through the gate and walked to the front door of the house. She turned and raised a hand in a wave as the little blue car drove off slowly. When it was out of sight, Zoe picked up her suitcase and walked back to the main street.

In the restroom of a service station Zoe stood in front of the grimy mirror and splashed cold water over her face before drinking thirstily from the tap. She took lipstick and eyeliner from her purse and made up her face.

A block away she came to the town's hotel, The Kruger, its white boxlike shape rising three floors above the quiet street. A limp flag hung over the entrance. Behind the hotel stood a garden, lush with the brilliant red of bougainvillea. The dark mountains towered over hotel and garden, reaching up into the grey clouds that obscured the summit. The air was damp with the promise of rain.

Zoe went through the heavy front doors and across the lobby to where a young man holding a paperback book close to his face sat behind the front desk. He looked up at her with an unfocused gaze when she set her bag down and tapped the counter.

"A room for the night, please."

His eyes came into focus. "Single or double?"

"Single, please."

"Just for yourself, is it, Miss?" His mouth with its thin fuzz of adolescent moustache began to form a smirk.

"My brother is meeting me here in the morning. He's a sergeant with the police." She glared at him until he flushed and dropped his eyes.

"Name and address here." He pushed a ledger and pen across the counter.

Zoe wrote down her name, hesitated for a moment, then filled in the address of her school. The boy leaned over and looked at what she had written.

"You have to pay in advance."

She selected two banknotes from her purse and dropped them on the counter.

When he had smoothed out the notes and given her the change he took a key from the wall behind the desk and laid it on the counter. "Second floor," he said, lifting his chin in the direction of the stairs as he retrieved his book. When Zoe walked across the lobby he leaned over the counter and watched the motion of her hips.

In her room Zoe sat down on the wide bed and unbuckled her shoes, then kicked them off and stretched back on the soft pillows. She heard the sound of water and closed her eyes, picturing the mountains above the town, with the dark volcanic rock spread high over the small white hotel far below. She saw ledges green with moss and hidden pools behind a sheer waterfall that tumbled down a precipice in a silent,

19

smoky vapour of cool mist...

It was dark outside when she woke and the room lay in shadow. She got up and turned on all the lamps, then went to the bathroom and washed the makeup from her face with hot water and soap. Draping her cardigan over her shoulders she locked the door and went downstairs.

The smell of overcooked roast beef and cabbage rose up to meet her when she looked in at the dining-room where only two of the tables were occupied and a bored waiter lounged next to the kitchen door. He glanced up expectantly at Zoe but she turned away and went out into the night.

The air was sweet and moist and she could hear the gurgling splash of a river, broken by the sharp, irregular call of a night bird. The few streetlamps cast weak pools of yellow-ish light at her feet.

Near the end of the street she heard music and saw the movement of figures silhouetted in the flow of light spilling from an open doorway. As she went nearer, the sweet night air was filled with the pungent odour of frying fish.

She soon came to the door of a fish-and-chip shop, where the light and warmth and cooking smell poured out into the night on a wave of rhythmic African music.

A big radio sat on the counter and next to it two men with their backs to her stood and watched the cook drop slabs of fish into a cauldron of sizzling oil. When he caught sight of her in the doorway the cook removed the cigarette from his mouth and turned down the radio. "Yes, lady?"

The two men looked at her, then stepped aside to make room at the counter. Zoe went forward, catching the sweetish tang of beer mingled with the smoky aroma of hot oil.

"One fish and chips, please." Her hunger was intense.

The cook made up her order first and the two men stood patiently in silence while she paid. With the warm newspaper-wrapped parcel in both hands, Zoe went outside and sat on the edge of the curb, just inside the rectangle of light from the open doorway.

It was her first meal of the day and she ate the greasy food in large bites, her eyes smarting from the vinegar and pepper on the chips.

The two men came out with their parcel of food and sat near her on the curb, talking softly in their own language as the music rose again in the shop behind them.

A warmth spread through Zoe's body as she sat there licking the remnants of oil from her fingers, tired but no longer hungry. The night was like a lullaby; the sound of the music, the men's voices rising and falling in rhythmic cadences, the air sweet and cool. She almost felt happy.

It was late when she woke to the milky light of midday in the room. She pulled back the curtains and looked down past the garden to a wide river. On the bank was a grove of orange trees and a little way beyond them a small white tent was pitched. A campfire sent a thin plume of smoke up to a sky heavy with grey clouds.

Zoe threw back the sheets and opened the window then leaned out on the sill. The drizzle was soft on her shoulders.

She ran hot water into the bathtub and lay there for a long time with the water up to her chin. Only when the bath was tepid did she get out and dress in front of the open window, her gaze fixed on the green river.

She asked for directions to Bella's house, then followed the path at the back of the hotel toward the river. She went carefully, mindful of her white socks and the clinging blackjack burrs that lined the path, until she was through the orange grove and on the riverbank where a narrow footbridge crossed the water.

The wooden planks of the bridge were slippery from the moisture-laden air and she held firmly to the handrail as the structure swayed slightly with her weight. The swollen river flowed below her feet, opaque and swift.

Over the middle of the river the bridge sagged down, almost touching the water and Zoe paused here to look back at the distant hotel, white against the dark mountains.

On the bank, near the tent with its lazy campfire, a man stood with a fishing rod. He raised a hand in greeting but Zoe looked away and went on.

By the time she reached the summit of the hill on the opposite side, the drizzle had turned to a steady rain and her hair was damp through, curling at the edges, her cardigan giving off the doggy smell of wet wool.

Bella's house was a plain white bungalow. After wiping her muddy shoes carefully on the mat and patting her hair into place as best she could, Zoe rang the bell. The door swung open almost immediately.

For an instant Zoe thought this must be Bella's mother. The young woman before her bore only a faint resemblance to the girl Zoe had sat with on the bus every morning.

The once demure hair was now swept up into an elegant wave that framed a heavily made-up face. Between fingers with bright red nails she held a cigarette with studied nonchalance. It was only the eyes under the blue-shaded lids that Zoe found familiar.

"Hello, Bella."

The girl stared at her blankly. Then a gradual expression of recognition came over her round face, followed by a look of naked dismay.

"Zoe! My God. What are you doing here?"

"I came to visit you, Bella."

Bella stared at her with incomprehension, the smoke from her cigarette drifting up like a veil between them.

"You came to visit me?"

"Yes. On the bus to Nylstad, then I got a lift."

"By yourself?"

Zoe nodded.

"On the bus?" Bella repeated and Zoe nodded again.

Suddenly aware of the rain blowing onto the porch, Bella stepped back a pace and touched a hand to her hair. "Well. This is a surprise. I suppose you'd better come in."

Zoe wiped her shoes on the mat again and followed Bella into the house.

"Actually, I thought you were someone else when I heard the bell ring," Bella said. "I'm expecting company at any moment."

Zoe hesitated at the edge of the pale carpet that covered the living-room floor. The room seemed like a picture in a magazine, everything new and spotless. She glanced admiringly at the long modern couch under the window, the glass coffee table, the tall floor lamps. And Bella standing there in the middle of the carpet, as glamorous as a film star in her white flared skirt with the red leather belt and matching high-heeled shoes.

"Your house is so wonderful," Zoe said, reaching out a hand to stroke the smooth leather of an armchair.

"Do you think so?" Bella asked in a pleased voice. "I helped Mother do all the decorating, although it's mostly my choices. Everything is new, from the catalogue at Barnett's." She stubbed out her cigarette in a wide glass ashtray and smiled at the room.

"It's so wonderful in here," Zoe said. She wished she had worn other clothes, and made up her own face.

"Come and see my room," Bella said. She took Zoe by the hand. "I'll show you my new dresses. They only arrived this morning." Her voice dropped a tone. "Everything around here is new since my dad left."

The bedroom had pink wallpaper and a pink cover on the bed. A mirror in an ornate gilt frame reflected a dazzling array of perfume bottles in neat order on the dresser. Zoe counted the bottles, twelve, as she ran her fingers across the glass, catching the sparkles in her hand.

Bella pulled open a closet and began to lay dresses on the pink bedcover. "Mother lets me order all the latest styles." She gave Zoe a mock grimace and added, "There isn't anywhere to wear them except to the dances at the hotel on Fridays."

Selecting a dress from the pile on the bed she held it up and inspected herself in the mirror. "What do you think of this one?" Without waiting for an answer she discarded it and selected another. "I don't know which one to wear this weekend."

"They're all so beautiful," Zoe said.

The doorbell rang. Two brief chimes, followed by two more.

"That must be Carl!" Bella said and flung the dress onto the bed. She bent to inspect her face in the mirror, baring her teeth once in a wide smile, then ran lightly out of the room. Zoe followed.

A young man with a sun-browned face and sandy hair stood leaning in the doorway. He wore jeans and a white shirt under a black leather jacket slick with rain.

"Hi, Babe," he said to Bella as he clasped her round the waist with one arm and kissed her on the mouth. Bella hung in his embrace a moment with her head thrown back, then laughed and pushed him away gently with her red fingernails spread across his chest.

He saw Zoe in the hall and winked at her. "Hi." His smile was brilliant against his tanned skin. Taking off his leather jacket he shook the raindrops away and handed it to Bella. "Who's your friend?"

"Oh, that's just Zoe. She dropped in for a few minutes." Bella turned to her. "This is Carl."

He hooked his thumbs in the belt at his waist and stared at her with a half-smile on his face.

"Pleased to meet you," she said and dropped her eyes.

Bella hung the wet jacket on a hook, then linked her arm through Carl's as she guided him into the living room. They sat down together in one corner of the long couch near the windows. Zoe slipped into an armchair across the room.

"How about a beer?" Carl said. He flashed a smile across at Zoe. "Want a beer, Zoe?"

She glanced at Bella. "Okay."

While Carl was in the kitchen Bella lit a cigarette and

patted her hair. Zoe looked out of the big window where the rain streaked across the glass like a curtain.

"He's nice," she said to Bella. "Are you engaged?"

Bella shrugged. "Oh, I don't know." She exhaled a thin stream of cigarette smoke. "Carl is fun to have around."

Carl returned with three bottles of beer. He stood just beyond Zoe's reach so that she had to half-rise and lean forward to take the bottle. When she looked up at his face he winked at her.

The beer tasted like metal and was too cold but she drank it down in quick swallows, suppressing a belch as she finished. Across the room Bella talked softly to Carl, her hand draped across his shoulder and her fingers toying with the curls at his neck.

A slackness spread through Zoe's limbs. She settled lower in the armchair and clutched the empty beer bottle between her hands. The beads of condensation on the outside of the glass were cool and moist in her palms.

Bella leaned forward and nuzzled Carl's neck with her red lips. Zoe watched with fascination as Bella's small pink tongue came out and flicked at Carl's earlobe, then her pointed white teeth nipped gently at the soft flesh.

Carl groaned audibly and pulled Bella into his arms.

When they emerged from their embrace Carl retrieved his beer and drained it with a sigh. He wiped the back of his hand across his mouth and looked at Zoe.

"Finished your beer already, Zoe? You must be a born drinker. Come on, Bella, drink up. Zoe is way ahead of us." He came over and took the empty bottle from Zoe's grasp.

Bella gulped down the rest of her beer. Her face was flushed and a smear of lipstick ran down from the side of her mouth.

Carl winked at Zoe and went into the kitchen. Bella lit another cigarette and smoked with quick puffs, blowing the smoke out in little sighs. She did not look at Zoe.

Carl came back and handed another bottle of beer to Zoe. She immediately took a deep swallow. "Hey, take it easy," Carl laughed. "That ain't lemonade."

He sat down next to Bella and whispered something in her ear. They both laughed. In a moment they were sprawled across the couch again in a tight embrace.

Zoe sipped her beer and watched the curtain of rain streaming down the windows. Her arms and legs felt heavy as lead. The afternoon seemed to be flowing past her in the dull grey light with the constant sound of falling rain. She was aware of her wet hands round the bottle and the sour taste of beer in her mouth. Bella and Carl were far away on the other side of the room.

She wished it was not raining and that she had her own house and that her hair did not look like a mess of twisted river weeds and that her clothes did not smell like a wet dog.

The corners of the room filled with aqueous shadows and Zoe had the sensation that she was sitting under water. Carl drifted by to bring her another bottle of beer and Bella smoked endless cigarettes. Nobody spoke and she felt herself to be almost invisible, sunk in the big armchair listening to the gurgling rain.

Suddenly Bella groaned, a sound like an animal in distress, and pushed Carl away. She got unsteadily to her feet and staggered to the centre of the room. Her face was pale and ghostly in the watery light and a faint sheen of perspiration glistened on her forehead.

"I must go to the bathroom," she announced and walked stiffly from the room with her head erect.

A door slammed and a moment later Zoe heard the spasmodic sound of retching.

Carl grinned and sat back on the couch with his arms spread.

"Bella can't take it, can she? Not like you, eh Zoe?"

He watched her for a long while in the dim light and she stared back, seeing only his bright smile.

After a time he patted the couch and said, "Why don't you come and sit over here?"

Zoe set her drink on the floor and crossed the room. The sluggishness in her arms and legs gave her the sensation of wading through water.

Carl sat up and took both her hands in his and slowly ran his thumbs over her knuckles. When he kissed her, Zoe shut her eyes and leaned back against the couch, tasting beer and faint tobacco.

A thin shriek pierced the air and Carl sprang away as quickly as if he had been burned. Bella stood in the doorway, a spectral presence with a damp and ashen face. Her mouth opened and emitted a plaintive wail.

"Christ!" Carl exclaimed as he crossed to her. "Take it easy, Bel. It was just a friendly little kiss."

Bella gave a choked sob and slumped against the wall, gradually sinking to the floor. Her shoulders began to shake convulsively.

"Come on, Bella," Carl said, hovering over her. "Come on now. It was nothing. Just a kiss. It meant nothing."

Zoe got up from the couch and edged past them to the door. She looked down at Bella and murmured, "Sorry," then she slipped out into the wet afternoon.

As she made her way down the hill the rain fell in a dense sheet that poured across her face and plastered her hair flat against her skull.

At the crossing she saw that the river had risen since the morning, overflowing its banks and surging across the boards of the footbridge. Zoe stepped up onto the swaying bridge and made her way over the current. The cold water washed over her shoes and up around her ankles.

In the centre of the bridge the handrail had broken loose and hung down in the water, swinging to and fro in the river like a beckoning arm. Zoe stopped here and looked down into the eddies where leaves and torn branches spun in rapid circles before being sucked below the surface.

A movement on the opposite shore caught her eye and she peered through the streaming rain to see the fisherman she had glimpsed that morning. He stood near the water's edge waving at her. Fool, she thought, what's he doing trying to catch fish in the rain? She looked away, up to the dark shape of the mountains, then turned her eyes to the black water washing over her feet.

A great weariness like a sleep came over her. She let all the muscles in her body go limp and toppled through the broken handrail into the river.

The water seemed to embrace her as she was dragged into the opaque depths. Darkness filled her eyes and ears. She opened her mouth wide and let the river draw her into a deep emptiness, turning and turning her away into the vast slow darkness.

It was night when Zoe opened her eyes. The rain had stopped and she could see the flickers of stars in a wide clear sky. Her chest hurt and she coughed once. A faint music seemed to wind between the stars like a liquid ribbon of light. Then the music faltered and died away. She strained to catch the melody again but it was gone.

She became aware of the hard earth beneath her back and the texture of a rough blanket drawn up to her chin. The music began again—thin clear notes moving through the air.

Zoe turned her gaze away from the open sky and sat up. A small campfire burned next to her and on the other side sat the fisherman she had seen so long ago. He was gazing into the flames while he played a small wooden flute.

He removed the flute and turned to regard her with dark eyes. Then an almost elfin grin spread across his mouth and he held the flute out to Zoe. She placed her fingers over the three holes cut into the soft wood and held the flute to her lips. She blew, hesitantly at first, then again with a longer breath, removing her fingers from the holes as she blew. A brief melody came to her ears and the figure across from her chuckled and nodded his head.

Zoe blew again and the thin questing notes rose above the

glow of the fire into the night. The fisherman sighed and stretched out next to the fire with his hands cradled behind his head and his face turned up to the stars.

Zoe played the flute again. The music came unbidden, formed she knew not where, flowing out with her breath into the night.

In the notes she heard laughter and songs and saw fields green with sunlight.

Zoe played on, letting the music flow out from deep within her and swirl through the darkness, the notes dancing with the red sparks of the fire, over the black river and across the sleeping town, past the high mountains and the long road across the flat dry country, onward up to the coloured light of the stars, going round and round, flying upwards higher and higher and higher.

A Visit to That Country

It's such a beautiful country, people said to Kate. That's what makes it all so tragic. Such a pity things have to be this way, they told her.

"Don't you think it's beautiful?" Dougie said. His wife nodded agreement. "I never get tired of the view."

Kate sat with them on the lawn outside their sprawling farmhouse in the late afternoon; the sun low over the eucalyptus trees in the distance, elongated shadows stretching across the lawn, the air cool with the scent of hibiscus and lemons after the heat of the day.

Their names were Douglas and Valery Parish. "Call us Dougie and Val," they said. "Everybody does. We don't stand on ceremony out here."

A servant brought a pitcher of brandy and soda on a tray, then moved away silently across the lawn.

"Have a sundowner," Dougie said, and poured Kate a drink. He settled himself more comfortably in his chair and took a sip from his glass, smacking his lips together in a little sigh of contentment. It occurred to Kate that he prided himself on his homespun manners.

"Peaceful, isn't it?" Dougie said with a sidelong grin, as if daring her to disagree. "This is basically a peaceful place, you know—despite what the newspapers write about us in your country."

Kate raised her eyebrows, but said nothing. She thought it best not to broach that particular subject. Dougie nodded and said, "Oh yes, we know what everyone thinks of us."

Kate shrugged.

Dougie regarded her a moment over the rim of his glass. "And what will you write about us?"

"I'm not really here to write about anything," Kate said. She worked for a nautical magazine and was in the country to cover a round-the-world sailing race that was due to make a stop at the southern cape. "I'm basically a tourist."

Dougie put both hands around his glass and smiled. "But you will write something. Won't you?"

Kate smiled in return. "Perhaps."

"Just don't get the facts wrong."

"What are the facts?"

Dougie looked at his wife, then back at Kate. "They're complicated. Most people get it wrong."

"I'm a travel writer. Politics is not my field."

"Good for you." He spread his arms in an expansive gesture. "Then you should write about this place—how beautiful it all is. Say something positive for a change."

Val leaned forward in her chair and said. "I think we're very lucky, to live out here in the peace and quiet of the country-side. Even if it does mean that Dougie has to drive an hour each way to the city every day."

"I'm only a weekend farmer, you see," Dougie said with a little self-deprecating shrug. "The rest of the time I have to work for a living. Not like some. But I love the land. I wouldn't move for anything."

Val gave her husband a sympathetic glance. "We're very fortunate," she said. "All our friends tell us how lucky we are. We have fresh eggs and vegetables, we don't have to deal with the pollution and crime in the city. And land is much cheaper here. I mean, look at what we've been able to afford." She raised a hand and waved it across the landscape. "People like us would never be able to afford a house like this in the city. We're not rich, you know."

Their house had many wide rooms with whitewashed stone walls under a high, thatched roof. The slate floors were always cool and the servants came and went on silent bare feet. The night before, during a thunderstorm, as Kate lay in bed and looked up past the broad exposed beams to the underside of the tightly thatched straw, she thought it seemed an inade-quate protection against the elements. Yet the thatch kept out the rain, and all she heard was a soft rustling above her head, like the whispers of distant voices.

"The house is modelled after a traditional native design," Val said.

"It's one of the few things the natives round here are actually good at," Dougie added. "Building houses, that is. Terrible farmers, though." He chuckled.

"I'm particularly fond of the roses this year," Val said. "It's amazing that they grow so well in such a wild place. The gardeners have done a superb job."

"And the fruit," Dougie said. "Peaches as big as your fist." He balled up his hand to show her.

Val nodded and said, "Every time we go home on a visit we're simply astonished at how small and sickly-looking the fruit is there."

"Home?" Kate said. She had understood that they were both born in the country—third-generation settlers.

"Just a manner of speaking," Val said with a little laugh and her hand fluttered across her mouth.

"She means the old country," Dougie explained. "This is home of course. Isn't it, darling?"

"Yes," Val said. "Absolutely."

Some distance beyond the gardens that belonged to Dougie and Val, past the sun-bleached fields of dry grass, Kate could see the pale smoke of cooking fires drifting above a collection of tin roofs.

Dougie's eyes followed the direction of her gaze. "There hasn't been much rain this year. But we've managed to keep the place up, keep it green."

"Who lives there?" Kate asked, pointing.

"Locals—farmhands, workers, that sort of thing. God knows who else. It's just a shanty town, not the sort of place you'd want to visit." He leaned forward and tinkled the ice in the jug. "Another drink?"

At the bottom of the garden, where an orchard screened the fields, a sudden flurry of movement interrupted the stillness of the view. A voice shouted, then the figure of a man in a vivid orange shirt broke through the screen of trees in a flash of colour. He glanced up at the house, then raced across the flowerbeds, running with a wild, forward-tilting motion, arms pumping, his head flung high. The orange colour of his shirt glowed against his dark skin in the soft afternoon light. Kate could clearly hear the gasping noise of his breath.

Two other men appeared immediately behind him; policemen in khaki uniforms, carrying their whips and hats in their hands as they ran. Their footsteps thudded across the grass.

Kate rose to her feet and moved quickly to the edge of the lawn. None of the men looked up at her.

A chest-high fence with a double strand of barbed wire separated the garden from the long grass of the uncultivated fields beyond, and for a moment Kate thought the fleeing man had not seen the fence. Then at the last moment, without breaking step, he leaped high into the air and sailed over the barbed wire.

Despite the violence of the moment, and the quick pulse of terror beating in her veins, as if her own heart had taken flight, Kate could not help but think of a gazelle in motion—one of those antelope that had darted out of the underbrush on the coast road and soared over the hood of her car with that same kind of terrified, yet effortless grace.

The two policemen reached the fence and climbed over the strands with difficulty. There was a curse as one of them snagged his tunic.

Dougie had come up beside her and stood with one hand in his pocket, twirling the ice in his drink so that it clinked against the glass.

Kate shot a glance at him. "Shouldn't we do something?"

"No need to. The police will take care of it."

She found his studied casualness strange. "Is this sort of thing usual here?"

Dougie shrugged and took a sip of his drink. "He probably didn't have any papers. Half the people round here don't have the proper residency permits. They just wander around as if they own the place. Happens all the time."

Val came up and stood close to her husband.

"Quite a jumper, eh?" Dougie said. "Too bad they didn't have a dog. They'd have grabbed him in no time."

Val turned to Kate with a small, apologetic smile. "I'm sorry you had to see that. It's one of the drawbacks to living out here. But what can you do? It's such a pity, really."

"A pity?" Kate said. "Is that what it is?"

She looked at the rather soft features of the other woman's face and noticed for the first time the hard glint in Val's blue eyes. She had thought of Dougie and Val as older than her—somehow she had pictured them as middle-aged from the moment she arrived at their house—but now she realised with a small shock that they were her own age, if not slightly younger. Her eyes met those of Val again, and the hardness frightened her. She wondered if it had been there all along, and whether she had merely failed to take note of it earlier.

Val said nothing. She stood with her hand resting on her husband's arm and stared back at Kate.

In the morning Kate took a train to the coast. She had been assured that it was the best way to see the country—the views would be magnificent, the journey luxurious.

She sat in the air-conditioned lounge car and watched the hot, dry landscape pass. The waiters wore white gloves and called her Madam as they replenished her iced tea. Sometimes the train stopped for no explicable reason and dusty, barefoot children would appear at the side of the track to gaze up at her with grave faces. When she raised her hand and pressed it against the window, the children did not acknowledge her wave.

On another occasion the train halted with a sudden jerk and a row of olive-green army trucks sped past the windows. Grim-faced young men with rifles between their knees stared at the train from beneath their helmets.

In the port city, at one of the receptions associated with the yachting event she was covering for the magazine, Kate met a young lawyer whose name was Alex Nathan. When she asked him about his job he told her he was active in what he referred to as "resistance politics." The passionate intensity with which he addressed her, coupled with an almost boyish vulnerability, charmed Kate. She accepted an invitation for the next day.

"I hope you don't mind me bringing the boys along," Alex said when Kate slid into the front seat of the Mercedes the following morning. He introduced the two small boys in the back as Bram and Piet.

"Not at all. I like children." She half-turned in her seat and smiled at the two boys. They had their father's looks. "Handsome boys."

"It's my turn with them this Sunday." He had told her earlier that he was divorced. "And it's a chance for them to see their brother." The occasion was a sporting event at his eldest son's boarding-school

They drove out of the city and past the affluent suburbs. "That's the mountain," Alex said, pointing. Kate bent her head and peered through the window. "When the clouds sit along the top like that, like a table cloth, you can see where it gets its name."

She thought about the first settlers who sailed into the bay under that picturesque mountain. If they could have foreseen the uncertain future they would bring to the country, might they have turned back? And the sailors on their round-the world-race, with this sight as their first glimpse of land after months at sea, would they be glad for a landfall here? Would they care about the troubled history of the country?

"This is the wine country," Alex said. The car was passing through long rows of vines. "I know a wonderful little inn that serves a terrific roast lamb. We might go there this evening?" He gave her a quick interrogative glance.

"I'd like that."

35

"We'll have some of the good wine. The stuff they don't send out for export."

He drove confidently, passing other cars with swift, decisive surges of speed. Kate looked at his hands on the steering-wheel, slim and well-cared for, and thought of Dougie, the way he had balled his fist up to show her the size of the peaches he grew on his land.

"So, what else have you seen on your trip?" Alex asked, interrupting her thoughts.

"I stayed a night at a bed-and-breakfast, near a town called Bellefontaine."

"I know the area," Alex said. "I had a case up there once. Beautiful place."

She told him about Dougie and Val, making it humorous, painting them as a ridiculous colonial couple. She thought Alex would appreciate the ironies. But when she recounted the incident she had witnessed, Kate recalled the look in Val's eyes, and the couple didn't seem quite as comical as she had intended to draw them.

"It wasn't their smugness so much that bothered me," she said, "but how unconcerned they were over what was really quite a frightening scene. That way that man ran—he was like a terrified animal. They didn't seem to care."

Alex nodded and glanced across at her. "But you really shouldn't jump to conclusions. The man might have been a criminal. You don't know what he'd done."

"If he'd done anything at all," she retorted.

Alex shrugged and watched the road.

After a while Kate said, "Anyway, my sympathies in a situation like that always lie with the pursued. Innocent until proven guilty. Isn't that what they say in your profession?"

"I suppose so," Alex said.

When they arrived, the cricket match was already in progress on a playing-field of manicured green lawn. The school had decorous stone architecture and a chapel with a high, Gothic spire. The cloud-draped mountains made a suitable backdrop.

Alex took a rug from the trunk of the Mercedes and spread it on the grass for her and the boys. "That's my son out there, Kevin. You'll meet him later. He's quite a good catcher." He watched the game a moment, then said to Kate, "I have to go and shake some hands, and talk to a few teachers. Kevin's having a bit of a hard time this year. Won't be long."

After half an hour, when Alex hadn't returned, and Kate was becoming bored with the game, she agreed to accompany the two small boys, who were equally restless, on a walk through the school grounds.

They skirted the cricket pitch and took her along a gravel path that followed a high, chain-link fence separating the school grounds from the untended countryside beyond. Everywhere in this country there were fences, Kate thought. The line in the dust was always clearly demarcated. But at least this one wasn't made of barbed wire.

The boys opened a gate in the fence and led her into the trees. In a moment they had reached the shelter of an abandoned orchard, where the low branches of the twisted trees were heavy with pale green fruit. "Those are wild quinces," Bram told her. "Don't eat them—they taste bad." He ran off into the trees with his brother.

The day was warm and Kate sat down with her back against one of the tree trunks. From the distant cricket match a soft pattering of applause drifted across the orchard. A wisp of breeze sighed over the grass. Cicadas murmured in the leaves. For a moment Kate felt she was experiencing the true, idyllic nature of the country, the one everybody talked about. She closed her eyes and dozed.

The excited voices of the two boys came from the other side of the trees, calling her name.

"Come quick, come quick!" Bram cried, when he caught sight of Kate. "There's a man. Lying in the grass."

"What man?" Kate glanced past him.

"Over there. He's lying down."

"Perhaps he's taking a rest."

"No," Bram said. He looked at her with the same solemn brown eyes that his father had and shook his head. "No, he is dead."

"He's not," the smaller boy said, but his voice quivered with doubt and he looked to Kate for reassurance.

"You'd better show me," Kate said.

They took her hands, one on either side, and led her forward in silence. After a few yards Bram released her hand and pointed. "There," he whispered. "I told you so."

Kate saw the man. He lay on his back with his hands folded neatly across his chest. His eyes were closed and his face was turned up to the sky. His body was absolutely naked.

Kate pulled the boys closer to her and moved back a few paces.

The man lay perfectly still. No rise and fall of breath moved in his chest, no tremor of awareness fluttered beneath the closed eyelids.

"See," Bram said, with a kind of grim satisfaction in his voice. "He is dead."

"Is he really?" Piet asked, looking up at Kate.

Bram bent to the ground and picked up a pebble. He flung it hard at the body. It struck the man on the chest and rolled away into the grass. Kate waited for some answering movement in that inert form.

How still the man lay, she thought. And how peaceful he looked; in such gentle repose, with the sun falling on the smooth brown skin, and the hands clasped together as if in prayer. She noticed how the long grass had been flattened by the weight of the body, how it spread around the man like a nest. He might almost have fallen from the sky, already naked and dead.

Piet, emulating his brother, scooped up a stone and flung it at the body.

"Stop it!" Kate said, and slapped at his hand.

It suddenly occurred to her that the man might not be dead,

that he might be ill, or wounded in some way. She crossed the patch of grass quickly and crouched down next to him. When she put her finger to his neck, the flesh was rubbery and cold. No small beat of a pulse answered her touch. Kate looked down at the expressionless face. A small black ant emerged from the cavity of the man's left ear and made its way across his cheek.

"What's the matter with him?" Piet called.

"He's dead," Kate answered.

"But why?"

Kate rose to her feet and looked at the faces of the two boys. "I don't know why." Such matters were beyond the realm of her experience.

"Come on," she said to the boys, glancing round at the trees. "We're going back." The orchard suddenly seemed a place of menace.

Kate found Alex amongst the spectators on the edge of the cricket field. "I've been looking all over for you," he said.

She drew him aside and told him what she had seen.

"Jesus," he muttered. "Are the boys all right?" He glanced down and reached out a hand to touch his sons.

"We're fine," Kate said.

"Okay, it's nothing to worry about. Wait here, and I'll take a look."

He returned some minutes later and went directly into the clubhouse without looking at Kate. When he reappeared he moved over to her and spoke in a low voice. "There's no need to mention this to anyone else at the moment. We don't want to disrupt the game. I'm sure you understand."

Kate was taken aback. "There is a dead man lying not a hundred yards from here. We should do something about it. At least call the police."

"I have called them. There's nothing more to be done. The police will take care of it. No point in spoiling the day for everyone, is there? It won't help."

Further conversation was drowned out by an eruption of

cheering and applause. The cricket match had ended. Evidently the home team had won.

"Look, I'll..." Alex said. He stared at her, then shook his head. "I'll be back in a moment." He hurried away to congratulate his son as the players streamed off the field.

Kate looked past the jubilant gathering of parents and boys to the distant grove of quince trees. It did not seem possible that a dead man lay there in the grass. It did not seem possible at all.

When she saw Alex again he was standing with his arm draped over his son's shoulders, the boy smiling up at his father with the flush of victory on his young face. The two of them laughed together.

A wave of hopelessness came over Kate, as if the apathy that afflicted the country had infected her too with its paralyzing inertia.

Kate remembered the man in the bright orange shirt who had run across that lovely garden like a frightened animal in the soft light of dusk. Was the culmination of that pursuit a death also? Another naked man lying dead somewhere in a field? Perhaps not that specific man. Any man would do. After all, the country did have a reputation for violence.

Kate turned and moved deliberately past the groups of celebratory parents and boys and made her way across the now-deserted cricket pitch. The green grass was soft as a carpet under her feet. She had almost reached the edge of the field when footsteps came running up behind her.

"Where are you going?" Alex said, panting slightly from his exertion.

"I want to know what happened," Kate said without stopping.

"Why? Why interfere?" He grasped her by the arm and she saw the resentment in his face. "What do you want there?"

"I want to know who that man was. I want to know his name."

"Look, these things happen." His voice strove to be reasonable. "There's no explanation. Not really. Don't you understand that?"

Kate shook off his arm. "That man had a name. Doesn't that mean anything to you? I'm not going to stand here like you, and Dougie, and all the rest of them, and sip my gin and tonic and shrug my shoulders and say, it's all such a pity, really, isn't it?"

Alex turned and looked back across the empty field to the school. When he faced her again his handsome features seemed to sag before her eyes. He stood like an actor who has suddenly forgotten his lines. And behind him the elegant stone buildings of the school were as insubstantial as a cardboard stage set.

"What an elaborate façade you've all constructed here," Kate said. "This sham architecture, your affluent suburbs and your fine wines, and all that talk about 'resistance.' Even the beauty that everyone goes on about is just a facade to hide the true ugliness." She took a deep breath and continued in a quieter tone. "Well, that man over there had a name once, a mother and a father, perhaps even a family. And I am not leaving this place until I can at least acknowledge that."

Alex stepped away from her. "You despise us, don't you? This whole country makes you feel self-righteously indignant, am I right?" Kate said nothing and he went on, "Well, now you have a little anecdote to take home with you. At your next dinner party you can entertain your liberal friends with the story of how you discovered a dead man that nobody cared about. You can impress them with how brave you were to want to find out his name."

Kate shook her head angrily and brushed past him. But he caught her by the arm again. "Let me ask you something. When you fly home to your own safe and free country, secure in your moral principles, where you can write indignant letters to the newspapers and boycott our wines, who is it that will remain behind? Who is it that will stand in court to protest the charges? Who is it that will visit the jails, and carry messages from desperate families? Tell me that much."

Kate looked past him and saw his three sons standing at the edge of the grass, waiting for their father. Beyond the orchard a grey police van had appeared and was bumping slowly across the fields.

"He is only one man," Kate said. "But we can't just forget about him."

When she looked at Alex again she was surprised by the shame and defeat that had come over his face. Kate felt a sudden rush of pity for him. Perhaps she had judged him too harshly. After all, she liked him, as a person, as a friend. It wasn't as if he were personally responsible for the death of that man lying in the grass.

"I'm sorry," she said. "I didn't mean.... Look, I know what it must be like, I understand what you have to go through." She reached out a hand and touched the sleeve of his jacket.

"No, you don't understand," he interrupted, brushing away her hand. "What do you know of this place?" He stared at Kate a long moment. "Who is it that will count the bodies?" he said. "And who will be called to account?"

He pushed past her and strode in the direction of the orchard.

Kate stood and watched his receding back. The long shadows cast by the low sun stretched across the field toward her, like black smears on the green grass. The chill of dusk was in the air and she huddled her bare arms close against her body. Then she set off toward the trees.

MURRAY LOGAN

Everett and Evalyne

The bus driver waits until I am seated before she pulls away from the curb. They're not supposed to do that, but some of them will. So that's a little gift, I suppose. She also calls me "dear," which is something else. She means well by it.

It's mid-morning and the bus is not at all crowded. Which means no-one feels obliged to stand, to give me his seat. I am always grateful when they do, who would not, but I always feel a certain—I don't know. As if something were being given and taken away at the same time.

Today is my birthday. I'm on my way to buy myself a birthday present. If you have no-one else to do it, then you do it for yourself. And now I am feeling sorry for myself. I will not feel this way. No-one likes a little old lady with a chip on her shoulder. Not even me.

I like to watch people, which is a blessing since I have no alternative to the bus. Not that I use it that often. I tend to stay in my own neighbourhood; I know all the little stores, a lot of the shopkeepers know me. A neighbourhood is like a little town, I imagine.

But today I am taking the bus downtown to buy myself a surprise. And on the way I watch the people on the bus. It seems that a different sort of person rides the bus these days. Everyone who can afford one operates a car, I suppose. You see teenagers—they're wearing their hair short again, which is a relief. Although that seems to upset a number of people, the very short hair. I think that it's a nice change from that hippy look you used to see. Perhaps it's the girls wearing it that way. It used to be that you couldn't tell if that young person with all the hair was a boy or a girl, and now it's the other way around. Still, I think that short is better than long. Cleaner, for one thing.

I get off the bus outside of Eaton's. As I walk along the side-walk I know that people, without even really looking, see what they want to see in me: another blue-haired old lady in crêpe-soled shoes. I know this. But I can't afford to slip and fall—I've seen the results. And would you rather see hair that is yellowed and stained, like the bottom of someone's ashtray? The blue keeps it neat. Although, I must say that I never thought I'd be one of them.

I know where the shop is, but I can't quite bring myself to go directly there. So I sit on a bench for a few minutes, enjoying the spring sunshine. I'm wearing one of those dresses you always see us wearing, as well. But what else could I wear? Slacks? A pair of jeans? Better to be quietly predictable than ridiculous, I think. Even if I didn't think, you can't escape who you are. You might not like it particularly, but there you go.

The beggars on the street bother me. Not for the reasons you'd think, but because I don't know how much I should give them. When the price of coffee is a dollar, should that be the correct amount? It seems like a lot to me, though. I drop a quarter into a man's hat and feel vaguely guilty all the way to the end of the block. And then I stand and fret, thinking that I should go back and give him something more. But the light changes, and I cross the street.

I stand outside the shop, fidgeting with my purse. The door, and the large window that faces the street, are frosted, so I can't see in. I read the sign again: Mother's Tattoos. I smile, mostly at myself. I'm not supposed to know that such places exist. I'm supposed to have spent my entire life knitting and putting up preserves.

I open the door and step inside.

It's like a doctor's. Chairs, a coffee-table, neat stacks of magazines. I cannot tell you the disappointment I feel. It's empty, but someone calls from the next room—a doorway is there, blocked off with a bamboo screen—telling me that he'll be right with me. I sit and look around.

The walls are covered with samples of tattoos. Sheets of paper or cardboard, each with a different design on it. I stand up and walk closer. Tigers, skulls, naked women carrying large swords that drip blood. Roses seem to be popular. I sit down again.

Two men come through the door, one of them hardly more than a boy. The boy, a teenager I suppose, leaves by the front door, so I am left alone with the other man. He's huge, tall and broad, though he's gone to fat as many of that sort do. He has long hair tied back in a pony-tail, and a beard that is mostly grey. He's looking at me as I'm looking at him. He's wearing a black t-shirt that says: Pig Iron Motorcycles—Fargo N.D.

"Pig Iron?" I ask.

He looks down at his chest, reading what is printed there. Does he not know which shirt he is wearing? "It's a motorcycle shop," he says. His voice has that bottom-of-a-barrel echo to it that big men get, but it's a pleasant enough voice. "Harleys." He looks embarrassed. "Harley-Davidsons; they're a kind of motorcycle."

"Yes," I say, "I know. My husband used to own one. A 1927 Harley-Davidson."

He smiles to himself. Here's an old lady making up stories, he's thinking. I can see him counting to himself, figuring things out. "1927?" he says.

"It wasn't new," I tell him. "I'm not that old, not quite. We owned it in 1943." I look around the room, letting him think I'm bored with this conversation. "I used to ride it a bit, but I never really got the hang of the stick-shift." Now he's taking me seriously. "I understand they don't use them any more," I say. "Modern motorcycles are different."

"No" he says, "they don't. Suicide shifts, we call them. And no, they don't use them any more." He nods at the bamboo screen. "Come in," he says, gesturing with one of his huge and, now that I notice, very tattooed arms. "Come in."

It's like I've passed a job application, or the first obstacle on a treasure hunt. I follow him around the bamboo screen and into the back.

You learn early that people have expectations. I was a schoolteacher, before I married my husband. Of course it was before I married my husband: only single women were allowed to teach school in those days. Single women of good character. And one day the superintendent of schools had a chat with me. I was summoned to his office for a friendly little chat. He couldn't help noticing that my lights were on, late at night. Sometimes very late at night, even midnight. Why yes, I said, yes, that's so. I read a good deal, and sometimes— It was expected that teachers of the children of our community do so with an alert mind and a rested body. The superintendent trusted that we'd have no more problems. We didn't. I sewed a thick set of curtains and did my reading in my kitchen, which didn't face onto the street.

The room reminds me, since I'm already thinking of one, of a kitchen. There's even a little half-fridge, tucked over in one corner. And, where I expected some sort of white-draped operating table or something, there is a red arborite table. The table is ringed with chrome and is the sister of one that sat in my kitchen for over 30 years before I gave it to the Salvation Army people. Instead of a G.E. toaster tucked over at one end, though, there is some other sort of machine, but it is chrome and rounded, and would not look all that out of place in my kitchen. The man is fiddling with something over by the sink.

"I'm making tea, would you like some?" he asks. I notice now that he has a bit of an English accent. Yes, I tell him, that would be lovely.

"Camomile okay?"

Yes, fine, fine, I say. He pours water into a kettle while I look around. I'm standing there, looking at the posters on the walls, mostly naked women on large motorcycles, when he suddenly remembers to offer me a chair. I sit down, and neither of us mentions the posters. I am pleased that he isn't embarrassed on my account.

I find the tea quite refreshing. It tastes of mint, and I quite like it. I don't know if I'll stop drinking the Nabob, but I quite like this. I started with Nabob when they had coupons in the boxes, and I've never switched. I don't think I ever bought anything with the coupons, come to think of it, but it's still a good tea. The secret is the pot, really.

"So," the man says, "what can I do for you, Mrs. . ."

"Prout," I tell him. "Evalyne Prout. And you are?"

He sips his tea, which he has in a large mug. He's given me an actual teacup. With a saucer, if you please. "They call me the Dutchman," he says. He looks slightly embarrassed, as much as a huge tattooed man wearing a black T-shirt can. "But my name is Everett, Everett Smythe."

"Well, I'm pleased to meet you, Mr. Smythe. But you don't sound Dutch to me, more like a Geordie."

I've surprised him, as his eyebrows rise by a quarter of an inch. "Newcastle-upon-Tyne," he says, "but that was a long time ago. You have a good ear, Mrs. Prout."

"Thank you, Mr. Smythe, I suppose I do." I look around the comfortable little kitchen area. "You need a cat."

He blows on his tea and then puts his mug down to look around, as if he expects to see one walk out from under the table. "Yes," he says, "I suppose I do. But it's not allowed. They have strict rules for tattoo parlours. I'm not really supposed to make tea in this area."

"No?" I say. "Well, that would be a shame, wouldn't it." And, the more I look around, the more the little space becomes a kitchen, the more we become two neighbours sharing a cup of tea in the afternoon.

When he makes another pot of tea he searches around for a bit and then presents me with a plate and two different sorts of biscuit. "Just like an old-fashioned English at-home, Mr. Smythe," I say, and he looks pleased. The chime from the door rings and he gets up and goes into the other room. I follow him and stand in the doorway while he asks a young girl with dirty blond hair for some I.D. She complains, but he doesn't seem to hear her. She tugs down her t-shirt to show her left shoulder—I can see a flash of colour and that's all—but Mr. Smythe shakes his head. Finally she leaves and we return to our tea and biscuits.

"How old were you when you got your first one?" I ask him.

He smiles and rubs at his forearm. "This one," he says, and rubs his thumb along a patch of faded blue. "When I was in the Royal Navy. I was sixteen and did it myself."

I lean forward and look more closely. It is, or was, an anchor, with some writing that I can't make out. The colour has faded to a grey-green, and the lines have smudged. It doesn't look like it was much to begin with. "You've gotten better since then, I hope?"

He laughs. "Yes, yes I have. And now Mrs. Prout, what is it that I can do for you?"

I tell him that I am 74 years old and that I have been widowed for 26 years. I tell him that I have no children, and I am increasingly frightened by loud noises, large strangers and change. My apartment smells of lavender and I don't know when I became old. I tell him it is my birthday.

"And now you want a tattoo," he says.

"And now I want a tattoo," I agree.

He nods his head, and his grey beard rises up and down, up and down his chest. He reaches out and takes another biscuit; he eats it, delicate bite by delicate bite, without saying a word. I sit and watch him, and I don't say anything either. I wish that there were a cat for me to pet.

I tell him that my husband worked at a sawmill on False Creek. Any number of jobs whose names changed as he made five or ten cents more per hour, until he lost three fingers from his right hand to one of the saws. After that they made him what you call an oiler. He was the one who went around making sure all the machines were lubricated, oiled. As far as I could tell that was the job they gave to someone they'd crippled but not quite killed. That's how it used to be. So I always had the thought in the back of my mind that he would go one day, victim of some kind of terrible and mechanical violence.

49

When it turned out to be his heart it was almost a relief. He had insurance, after a fashion, and that was that. All of a sudden I was living alone in a too-hot apartment in Kerrisdale, and people were giving me African Violets. I look at Mr. Smythe as if I expect him to understand all of this.

"Look, Mrs. Prout. . ." he says. He has spread both his hands wide, their palms up, and is looking from one huge hand to the other. As if the words he were trying to find were carried in either the left or the right. "Mrs. Prout," he says again, and I pick up my teacup, though I know full well that it is empty, and sip from it. I place it back on its saucer and look him in the eye. "Mr. Smythe," I say.

Mr. Smythe sighs. He turns his hands over and grips the edge of the table, pushing himself to his feet. He clears away the cups and the plate and then stands, looking down at me. "Have you ever done this before?" he asks.

"Have I ever. . .?"

"A tattoo, Mrs. Prout. Have you had a tattoo done before?"

I look down at my arms, sticks covered in translucent skin and thin blue veins; now it is I who am looking to find something. "No, Mr. Smythe, I have not."

He sighs again. "And now you've decided that you'd like one, as a sort of—"

"Birthday present," I say, before he can. "Yes, Mr Smythe, that is exactly what I would like. Do you think that you can do that for me? That is what you do, isn't it?"

He nods, his face stern behind his beard, under his hair, a pink dot in a cloud of grey. "First I'm going to have to see some I.D.," he says.

All the way home, on the bus, I burn to touch it. I sit, with my hands folded on my lap, and I burn. I smile softly to myself and I wonder if people can tell. Would they say, should they notice, that something is different about me? Would they wonder what it is, what has this old lady done that makes her smile like this? A thin boy with messy hair stands beside my seat, and I see, stencilled into the pale skin of his upper arm, the cartoon of a young girl holding an ice-cream cone. And I feel that we have a secret between us, we two, and he doesn't even know it. I smile, I beam at the boy, but he doesn't notice. It is enough that I know.

Looking over my shoulder into the mirror, I can see the gauze. Mr. Smythe has told me to leave it on for three days, not to wash it, and then it can come off. My left shoulder-blade is the location we finally decided upon, and I look at it now in the mirror. The gauze will come off but I still won't be able to see it, he's said. There will be a scab, and I am not to touch it. I must wait until it comes off by itself, piece by piece. Bit by bit I will see what he has drawn on my skin. He has warned me that if I have second thoughts then, it will be too late. He has told me there will be no going back, and I have told him I will not want to. Still, he tells me this again, stresses the permanence of what I am about to do. I tell him I am ready. I tell him I feel as if I were seven years old, and it is early Christmas morning.

And, of course, I can't keep a secret. I had intended to, I truly had. My present to myself was to have been a surprise that I wouldn't see: when I am gone, and am being laid out, wouldn't everyone be surprised to see what was there, etched on my left shoulder-blade. Who would have thought, I imagine them all saying, isn't that the strangest thing.

But, I find that I can't. I tell myself that I won't, as I am on the phone inviting my friend and neighbour Irene to come to tea. I tell myself that I can resist, as I am laying out the seed cakes and putting the water on to boil. And then the buzzer rings, and I know that I will tell all. And I am glad.

Irene spills her tea. Irene actually spills her tea when I tell her. "Wait, wait," she says. "Start over, start from the very beginning. I want you to start from the very beginning."

"Well," I say, "I decided—"

"Who would have thought? Who would have thought?

Now start over, start right at the very beginning."

"*Well*," I say...

He wore pale yellow rubber gloves. The needles came out of a sealed package, I remember him using his teeth to tear a corner of it and thinking: that's probably not right. The needles fitted into a shiny steel appliance with a long black electrical cord. He plugged it into the same socket that he'd used for the kettle. He swabbed my shoulder-blade with alcohol. I could smell it in the air, and my skin felt cool as it evaporated.

We'd decided that my shoulder would be the best. Mr. Smythe told me that he's done them everywhere. Everywhere. He blushed when he said it, not something you'd expect him to do. I told him that my shoulder would be fine.

He drew the outline with a felt pen. He showed me the pen, and it was like one a schoolchild might carry in her pencil-case. He told me that he draws free-hand and, to tell you the truth, he seemed quite proud of that fact. I hadn't really considered that there was any other way to do it.

The machine buzzed and vibrated; it sounded for all the world like a neck massager I used to have. That I probably still have, somewhere. It stung, but not as much as you'd think. It hurt, but the hurt slowly moved as he carefully traced what he had drawn, and it wasn't so bad, not really. All in all, it wasn't so bad.

But what is it, what is it? Irene wants to know. I nibble at a corner of my seed cake, take a sip of my tea—how many cups have I had today, I wonder—and look Irene square in the face. "I don't know," I say.

"I beg your pardon," says Irene.

"I don't know," I say again. "I let him choose." I smile sweetly at Irene. "I told Mr. Smythe that I wanted to be surprised."

Irene phones or drops by several times a day after that. "Anything yet?" she asks, and I must tell her no, no, there is nothing yet. The gauze comes off, but there is still nothing to see. Even so, I pull the neck of my dress off my shoulder to show Irene. She leans in close, trying to see beneath the crust of dried brown blood.

"It's not very big," she says.

"No, it's not," I say. I too had expected it to be larger. I've decided that Mr. Smythe must have known best, though. He'd thought for a long time, when I asked him to do it. He'd tried to talk me out of it, giving me one reason after another, but I was resolute. So he must have made the right choice. Irene is burning with curiosity, and for some perverse reason this makes me act as if I were bored, completely bored with the whole affair.

"I suppose we'll know what it is, soon enough," I say. And when Irene is gone I stand in front of my mirror trying to imagine what it is that is forever traced into my skin.

The doubts begin to come just when the scab is breaking away. What if it is something obscene; worst of all, what if it is completely banal? What if, rather than the thing of tiny beauty I've imagined, it is clumsy and gross? What if, what if? I remind myself that I am a good judge of character, and that Mr. Smythe would do no such thing. I tell myself that I have made my bed, and now I will lie in it, no matter what shape it may be.

And still I worry, as I wait for the flakes of my dried blood to crumble and fall away. What was I thinking? When people find out, they will laugh at me. What was I thinking?

I was thinking that I wanted to do something and I did it. I was thinking that, just because I'd been one way for 74 years, day in and day out, doesn't mean that one spring day I can't be something else. I look at my reflection in the mirror, eye to eye with this face I have watched change, this hair that I've watched go from black to grey to blue, and I nod my head. I nod my head and I smile.

I almost miss my stop. I've been sitting, hands clasped together, staring into space and when I look up I see that the bus has arrived. I see the Eaton's building and must struggle to get to the doors and down the steps before the bus leaves. It groans away, and I am left standing still on a sidewalk that is nothing but people hurrying from one place to another. I square my shoulders and begin to walk.

I walk right up to the door and open it. I hear the buzzing of his machine coming from the next room, and I sit down. I don't read a magazine, I don't look at the posters and samples on the walls. I sit and I wait.

They are finished soon. I don't even notice the man who opens the front door and exits. I am waiting and watching to see Mr. Smythe's face. "Good day, Mr. Smythe," I say.

He nods when he sees me. Of all the things I'd imagined he'd do, this is not one of them. He nods, and then gestures with his arm. "Hello, Mrs. Prout. Won't you come in?"

He puts the water on to boil, and then he sets a plate of biscuits in front of me. "You seemed to like these the last time," he says. "I bought some more."

I glare at him, but he has turned back to fool with the teapot. "No, thank you, Mr. Smythe," I say.

"Well, I'll just leave them there," he says. "Just in case." And then he comes back and sits down at the table with me. He reaches and helps himself to a biscuit, eating it with tiny bites, afternoon tea with the Queen.

"You know why I am here, Mr. Smythe?"

He nods again, his beard rising and falling on his t-shirt. This one is white and reads: Hog Heaven, Harleys Forever. I want to ask him if all of his clothing pertains to motorcycles, but I do not. I reach for a biscuit and then I pull my hand back. "Mr. Smythe—"

He stands suddenly. "There's the kettle," he says, though we both know it hasn't had time to boil. While he is fussing with the tea I eat a biscuit.

Finally he sits down again. "Now, Mrs. Prout," he says.

"Yes, Mr. Smythe. Now."

And then we sit, neither of us saying a word. We sit long enough for the tea to steep, and so Mr. Smythe pours each of us a cup.

"May I show you something, Mr. Smythe?" I don't wait for an answer. I put down my teacup and undo the first two buttons of my dress. I pull the material down over my left shoulder and twist to show it to Mr. Smythe. "Tell me what you see, Mr. Smythe."

He is fidgeting, his big hands opening and closing. On one arm the tattoos end at the wrist, like the cuff of a red and blue patterned shirt. The other has the back of the hand thickly tattooed, though I can't tell what the pictures are. "Mrs. Prout," he says, his hands moving.

I still hold the material of my dress down, and now I turn my head and look down at my shoulder-blade. "I'll tell you what I see, Mr. Smythe, I don't see anything at all."

"Mrs. Prout."

"I see nothing, Mr. Smythe, just a fading outline of a cruel joke. Is that what you see? I'd like to know, Mr. Smythe, is that what you see?"

When the scab first flaked away, bit by bit, and all I could see was the thin red outline, I thought that must be how it is. Maybe it takes a few days for the colour to come up, I thought. That must be how it is, and everyone knows it. Silly of me not to.

But then, once all the dried blood had peeled off, I was left with nothing but the thin outline of a teacup and saucer. I thought that quite sweet, a delicate teacup, outlined in red. But, after a few days, even that faded away. Until I was left with the faintest of ghost images, and the knowledge that I'd been had for a fool.

"Now, Mr. Smythe, shall we try it again?"

He takes a bite of his biscuit and then a sip from his mug of tea. When he smiles his teeth seem bigger and whiter than they should be. "Whatever you say, Mrs. Prout. Whatever you say." And this time I watch him take up the little vials of ink, the ink that will make whatever he draws permanent.

He is just leaning in to begin work when he stops and pulls away. "Mrs. Prout," he says, "I'd like to make one thing clear." I stare straight ahead, reading the neat labels on his tins of tea, coffee, sugar. "What I did wasn't intended as a joke, it was—" I turn to look at him and I see that this is not easy for him. Good, I think to myself. He stands, holding his tattoo apparatus, not quite meeting my eye. "I wanted you to be sure, Mrs. Prout. I wanted you to have a second chance." He's speaking in a strangely formal way, like a child in front of a Principal or Minister. "I'm sorry if that hurt you. It was not intended to." My eye has wandered, but now I study this bear of a man, his mass of hair and beard, his tattoos. I listen to his voice, the faint accent that he's carried with him despite all his changes.

"I understand, Everett," I say, and I believe that I do. "Please," I add, "you may call me Evalyne."

When he is finished and the gauze is on, we wait for another pot of tea to brew, one that is properly made this time. He and I are same in this, in our faith in tea, in the simple rituals of biscuits and good china for guests. And I smile to think that I have such a thing in common with such a man. Finally, when I can endure it no more, I ask him what he has drawn.

"Evalyne," he says, "you'll just have to wait."

Oh, Henry

"This might get a little weird," Sharon says. "So I want to thank you now for coming with me." They're sitting together in the back of Sharon's mom's old car. Sharon's mom is driving and the seat beside her is filled with a huge suitcase, so Sharon and Rowena hunch together in the back like two eight-year-olds. Sharon talks in a normal voice, not at all concerned that her mother can likely hear.

"Very weird," Sharon says. "Just so you understand." She pats Rowena on her knee, thanks, then goes back to watching her mother guide the car down the road. She does this so intently it's as if the force of her will alone keeps the car out of the ditch.

Rowena doesn't understand a thing, actually. She hardly knows Sharon, doesn't know Sharon's mother at all, isn't sure she wants to. She's known her for all of about eight minutes, the length of time they've been driving this car. At about minute-five Sharon's mom had grunted, the first noise she'd made, and said, "Rowena, huh?"

Rowena told her, yes, Rowena, and had leaned forward, ready for whatever came next.

"Huh," Sharon's mom had said. Then again, "Huh."

Sharon and Rowena work together at Beeker's Insurance, Rowena just for the past four months, since her divorce and everything that entailed, Sharon forever as far as Rowena can tell. Sharon is pretty down on Beeker's, but Rowena likes it. It's only been four months though, so you can't really tell.

One of the things she likes is what you get to find out. All those files, all those lives. One of those lives, one life in particular, was Sharon's dad. Claim disallowed: suicide. So that was something else, sharing the back seat with them, Sharon, Rowena and Sharon's disallowed father. Huh.

The car rattles along, Sharon's mom humming to herself, Sharon leaning to watch over her shoulder like a kid. Rowena beginning to wonder if maybe something is a little wrong with the whole family. Which makes her think about the disallowed dad and how he did it. They don't put things like that in the files, though. Maybe it was in this very car, who knows? Rowena runs her fingernails over the worn red vinyl of the seat. Sharon is still staring down the road and so doesn't see when Rowena pushes one nail through, a dagger thrust in and out.

Sharon's mom turns a corner and the car feels like it's going to flip over. They can't be moving faster than twenty miles an hour, but the shocks are so bad that Rowena slides clear over next to Sharon, who doesn't seem to notice but gives Rowena a little bump with her hips, oomph, and puts her back in place. Rowena is beginning to think that Sharon's dad did the right thing.

But still. Sharon is her only friend in this town, if you want to call what they share a friendship.

"What?" says Sharon's mom.

"Nothing," says Rowena.

"It's always something," says Sharon's mom.

"Not this time."

Maybe there's something wrong with the whole town. Rowena didn't exactly research the place before she moved. Just picked it more or less at random and then set out. No, that's wrong. She picked it exactly at random, like in the movies, like you're supposed to do when you start a new life. Open a map, close your eyes and drop a finger. Next time, she'd peek. These things only work out in the movies. In real life you wind up...well, you wind up exactly where she is now.

Sharon is pointing, her arm wobbling in front of Rowena's face like a plate of Spam. Which is not a nice thing to be thinking and is not at all fair to Sharon. Look at her mom, for instance, and you'll know she never had a chance. Rowena is, of course, ashamed of this thought. But she's also a little bit thrilled. Part of it is the flat out pettiness of it, but part of it is relief that, no matter what else goes wrong for her, she's still better off than Sharon and her Spammy arms. Pretty much, when you add everything in.

"There," Sharon says, "that's where we're going." The road, which has been running more or less straight through farmers' fields and thin woods, makes a hairpin curve up ahead. On the other side of the curve, just opposite them, is where Sharon is pointing.

Rowena squints. "A graveyard?"

"Dad," says Sharon and nods her head. Mom doesn't say anything, just gives the old car more gas and Rowena gets ready to die half-way through the turn.

Sharon's mom parks the car on a section of gravel that lies just through the gates. When Rowena gets out she sees that there's a lot of oyster shells mixed in with the gravel. Probably the bleached white looked really nice at one time, but now not so much. It's a nice touch though, not something Rowena would have expected.

Like she wouldn't have expected Sharon's mom to become all talkative, but she has. Something about where they are maybe, or she's warming up to the idea of Rowena coming along for the ride, who knows? But she certainly is talking.

"Three years," she says, like this means something. Then, when nobody says anything, Rowena because she doesn't know what's going on, Sharon because she is now pointedly ignoring the whole situation, she says it again. "Three years. To this very day." And she smiles at Rowena and then opens the passenger door and tries to wrestle the suitcase out.

"He did it three years ago to this very day," she says, tugging on the suitcase that has wedged itself between the seat and the dashboard. And Rowena suddenly knows what she's talking about. She panics a little when she realizes that she's going to hear all about it, there's no way around it, and looks to Sharon for help. But Sharon has walked away from the car, her steps making determined scrunching noises in the gravel and shells, then no sound at all as she walks away over the too-long grass that surrounds all the markers and stones.

Sharon's mom is cheerfully wrenching on the suitcase—
what is *in* that thing?—not twisting it or moving it to try a
different approach like you'd expect a normal person to do,
but simply tugging on its handles and cramming it tighter
and tighter into the bind it's in. She smiles at Rowena, stopping her efforts for a second and actually gasping for breath.
"They never found the body, you know."

What? "Here," says Rowena, "let me help you with that."
Which makes Sharon's mom beam. A very pleasant-looking
woman, really, despite the family arms, probably in her early
sixties with home-permed hair and a cardigan sweater over
her best dress. Crazy as a loon, thinks Rowena, but pleasant-
looking.

The case is heavier than it looks and bumps against
Rowena's leg as they follow after Sharon. Ahead, Sharon is still
ignoring them, the graveyard, the birds that scream at her
from the fir trees that surround the area, everything. Which
doesn't seem to bother her mom, so Rowena figures it's best to
let it go. Besides, by now she's burning to know what, exactly,
is in this case she's carrying. Curiosity, that's a failing with her,
she's been told that, she was always one to know a secret.

Which has a lot to do with what she's doing here at the
graveyard. And here in this little town for the past four
months. She never could let well enough alone, she always had
to get to the bottom of things. Which on the one hand means
humping this case over hill and dale so Sharon's mom can do
who knows what at the empty grave of Sharon's disallowed
father.

And, on the other hand, it meant staking out her husband
thinking she'd catch him in bed with a seventeen-year-old
named Tiffany with too much jewellery and breasts up around
her collar bones. But there was no Tiffany, at least none that
she could discover. Not that she didn't keep trying. Or any
other reason that her husband would admit to. He just left,
goodbye, so long, and that was it. And how are you supposed
to deal with a thing like that?

Maybe it's a trombone, or a tenor sax like she wanted to play in the high-school band until they talked her into the clarinet. Tenor saxes were supposed to be for the boys. Maybe Sharon's mom had held out against them. Maybe she is going to play some kind of soulful jazz piece over the blank grave of her three-years departed husband. Rowena looks around. Theirs is the only car nosed in on the gravel and oyster shell, no-one else is in sight amongst the headstones. What the hell, let 'er rip.

If that's what it is. Now she is really burning for some answers. And what did she mean they never found the body? Where was it and how did he, you know, how did he do it? Questions, questions. Curiosity can be a terrible thing, she thinks, and switches the case to her other hand. Sharon's mom has got ahead of her and Rowena has to hurry to catch up.

Sharon is waiting for them. "Come on," she says, gripping Rowena by the arm, the one carrying the suitcase. Rowena looks and sees that Sharon's mom has stopped and is looking down at a stone rising out of a clump of too-long grass. That must be where he is, she thinks. She reconsiders. That must be where he would be, if he were here. Then Sharon is tugging harder on her arm and they move away. "We'll leave her alone for a few minutes," Sharon says. "Besides, it gives me the creeps."

There's a path that runs around the edge of the cemetery and they walk on that. Rowena hadn't thought to put the suitcase down, so now she has to carry it with her. It's heavy, and getting more so the more they walk. She'll have a bruise in the morning the way the thing is slapping against her leg. Sharon either doesn't notice or won't comment on the suitcase. Rowena switches it from side to side, stopping each time to do so, but Sharon just stops right along with her and doesn't say a word. It's driving Rowena nuts.

But now Sharon has decided to talk. "It's been three years," she says, not looking at Rowena, "three years to the day since he did it." Yes, yes, thinks Rowena, I know that.

"He took a ferry to the mainland and halfway across he jumped over the side." Sharon doesn't look at her as she says this.

"He jumped over the side," Rowena repeats, like an idiot, but what else is she going to say? She doesn't have a lot of experience with conversations like this. And then Sharon starts to laugh, starts to laugh really quite hard, and Rowena is a little concerned that she'll become hysterical.

But, no, Sharon is just fine. "Actually," she says, and now she's once more straight-faced and looking at Rowena in all seriousness, "he hopped." Rowena doesn't have the slightest idea what she's talking about, but she'll be damned if she asks. She can be as stubborn as the next person, as the next two people, even if those two people are Sharon and her mom.

They round the last curve and head back toward Sharon's mom and the grave. It's a small graveyard. Rowena's waiting for Sharon to say more, but Sharon doesn't appear to be in any hurry. Is it really a grave, Rowena wonders, when there's no body? They're almost there; Rowena's mom hears the sound of their feet on the gravel and looks up. She reaches for the case and Rowena, inexplicably, feels a slight pang at having to give it up.

"I hate this," Sharon says. Her mother doesn't seem to hear her but is bent over the case, lying on its side, opening the big brass snaps that hold it closed.

"I really hate this part," Sharon says again. She grabs Rowena by the arm and pulls her back, away from the grave and Sharon's mom.

"What's going on?" Rowena whispers, giving in, okay, they win. Her voice sounds like a hiss in her own ears. "What's she doing?"

Sharon is rolling her eyes. "He went down to the car deck in the middle of the crossing and took off all his clothes." One of the snaps is stuck, or locked, and Sharon's mom is jiggling it back and forth. If she can hear Sharon she gives no sign.

"He took off all his clothes, piece by piece, and folded them neatly and put them on the floor."

"Someone saw him?" Rowena asks, details suddenly important.

"No, no one *saw* him," Sharon says, rolling her eyes at Rowena now. "They found his clothes, all in a neat little stack, everything folded—jacket, shirt, undershirt, pants, underpants and socks—all in a neat little pile on top of his shoes." The way she recites this list makes Rowena again wonder about the sanity of the whole family. There's something a little...obsessive about the whole crew.

Sharon's mom manages to pry the lid of the suitcase off. Okay, thinks Rowena, now we'll see. I wonder what song she'll play. She considers. What if they're required to sing along?

Sharon digs her fingers into Rowena's arm. She speaks quickly, her voice insistent. Her eyes are just a little bit wild, like she is in a race to tell something to Rowena before her mom can finish whatever it is she's doing.

"He left it all stacked in a pile, neatly folded." This is supposed to mean something but Rowena cannot imagine what. Then, watching her mother, who is still inexplicably bent over the open case, Sharon whispers, "It must have been very cold on the deck. The wind, the steel deck under his foot as he balanced there."

Rowena nods her head, though she has no idea what is happening here. "He weighted it all down," Sharon says, "to keep the clothes from blowing away. He didn't leave a note, nothing, but he made sure that his clothes weren't swept away." Maybe Sharon is beginning to cry, but maybe not. Rowena can't tell. This is not what she'd expected; this is nothing like anything she's done before. "And," says Sharon, "he weighted it down with that." Rowena looks and Sharon's mom has finally finished with the case. She stands and holds in her arms, cradles in her arms, an artificial leg.

Rowena feels like she's received a hammer blow to the forehead. She stands, gaping at this impossible image—Sharon's mom is now propping the leg so that it stands disembodied over the grave—and everything disappears, rushes away from her, until all that is left is an overwhelming feeling of pity and love for this woman she has known for less than an hour.

Sharon grabs her by her arm and wrenches her away. "Come on," she hisses. Then again, "Come *on*." She frogmarches Rowena away and they're off walking the path again, leaving Sharon's mom to whatever it is she's doing.

"It's like she thinks he'll come back or something," Sharon says, then trudges on.

Rowena can't be sure that she's not talking to herself. "Pardon?" she says, and trots for a few feet to catch up. Sharon's walking quickly and they're already up to the first curve. Rowena wonders if this is part of the routine, if Sharon does this every year.

"She thinks he'll what?" she says, priming Sharon, caught up in all of this now, as much a part of it as either of the other two women. "She thinks he'll come back?"

Sharon stops dead in her tracks and Rowena almost crashes into her they'd been walking that fast, almost running. Sharon jerks her head back toward her mother who is, Rowena sees, simply standing there, the third in a line of objects: gravestone, leg, Sharon's mom. Rowena realizes that all this time she's been thinking of this woman as Sharon's mom. She tries to conjure a name for her, an identity that belongs to her and her only, no need for relationship, no need for anyone else. She can't do it and, besides, Sharon is talking again.

"It's like bait, you know? Like once a year she figures she has a chance to get him back, that if she just waits long enough, he'll return to get his..." She trails off, and Rowena isn't exactly sure why. Maybe she can't bring herself to say the word "leg," maybe she's all upset again. Rowena can't say. Sharon grabs her by the arm again, Sharon is certainly fond of arm grabbing, that's one thing she can do, and jerks Rowena off the path. They're at the opposite end of the graveyard from Sharon's mom, the woman with no name, though it's such a tiny place that Rowena figures she could toss a pebble and hit her. Maybe toss a larger rock and knock over the leg. Win a prize. She shakes her head to stop these kinds of thoughts. She has the vague sense that she's with the wrong person, that alliances have been drawn up and she's on the wrong side.

Sharon sits down on the grass, her back against a head stone. Rowena has no choice, she sits down too, though she's careful not to sit on top of anybody. It's not that she's superstitious, or even religious, it's just a matter of good manners. The same reason she got caught up in all this insanity in the first place.

Sharon lights a cigarette and jams the smouldering match into the grass beside her. Great, thinks Rowena, and where is she going to put the butt when she's done? Now she has something else to worry about, something else that is none of her business.

"You were married, right?" Sharon says. Rowena notices that she's careful not to blow smoke at her, so that's something, anyway.

"Right," Rowena says. "I was married." She looks around, as if they're at some scenic vista somewhere. Trees, grave-stones, some dirty oyster shells. She doesn't look to see what Sharon's mom is doing.

"And?"

"And I don't want to talk about it."

Sharon puffs on her cigarette, thinking about this. Then she flicks the ember off the butt and wraps what's left in a Kleenex. Rowena watches her tuck the Kleenex into her pocket, slightly surprised, but Sharon doesn't notice.

"I'd like to have an ex-husband," she says, leaning back against the headstone.

"*What?*" Rowena quacks, surprised yet again.

"I think it would be nice to have an ex-husband, a past that's nicely wrapped up and cut off. Something you can hand people in a neat little package. I think you're actually lucky, when you think about it."

This is the first time that Rowena has been told she's lucky, and she does have to think about it. She's never felt sorry for herself, but she's hasn't exactly been overjoyed, either. One thing, she'll be lucky if she gets out of here pretty soon. She's done her bit for friendship, even one as brief and as thin as the one she and Sharon have, and now she'd just like to go.

But Sharon isn't done with it. "Because that's more than I have," she says, "something that I can hand out to explain who I am and where I'm at." She gets to her feet, pulling herself up by leaning on the headstone. Rowena stays seated, looking up at her. "And it's certainly more than my mom has, if you want to look at it like that. All she has left is—" and she jerks her head toward her mother and the leg. Rowena doesn't bother to look; it's like the leg has begun to fill the whole clearing, suffusing everything. Even with her eyes closed, she thinks, all she'll be able to see is the leg. "That's not something you can give to people," Sharon says, "it's worse than nothing at all." And then she turns and starts walking again, crunching along the oyster path.

Rowena gets up herself and walks back to the grave. Sharon's mom smiles at her, then goes back to staring at the leg and, just behind it, the grey stone marker. Rowena sees that Sharon's father was named Lloyd, and that he was born in 1932. Nothing on the stone says anything about when or how he died.

She looks at the leg. It's one of those objects that looks familiar, even if you've never seen one before. There is no possibility of it being anything other than what it is, just exactly what it is, right now.

Sharon's mom has propped it against the headstone. If Sharon's dad were sitting on top of the stone, facing them, the leg would be in just that position. Its thigh at an angle to the stone, the leg sloping to the knee, and the knee bent so that the lower leg and foot meet the ground at close to a right angle. Rowena can practically see Sharon's ghost dad, perched there, casual, connected to the ground by that one leg.

The leg is a cream colour, its skin a smooth rubber or plastic. Rowena has a brief urge to roll up a leg of her pants—she checks and sees that it would be the left one—to compare. But hers would have nubs of hair, some veins showing here or there, maybe a scratch on her shin from hitting the edge of the coffee table. She looks at her hands, front and back, to check the skin colour, and that would be wrong too. She is too pink, for one thing. And then there are bumps and ridges, lines, pale blond hairs, an endless list of complications.

The leg is shoeless, and she wonders about that. Maybe, she thinks, Sharon's mom wants it left just the way it was...at the end. The foot has no toes, she notices.

Sharon's mom coughs. Rowena is standing right beside her, shoulders almost touching, so when she coughs again they bump together, once, twice, like dolls on the same string. Neither of them moves, but Sharon's mom begins to speak.

"I have this dream," she says, but that's all she says, like Rowena is supposed to know what she means. Rowena keeps staring at the stone and at the leg, at Lloyd's leg. She knows the name of Sharon's disallowed ghost dad, but the woman next to her, the woman close enough to bump into her when she coughs, is only Sharon's mom.

"I have this dream," she says again, after a bit, and of course Rowena knows what's coming, more or less. "Where he's swimming, swimming away. And he has two legs. He's a good swimmer, a strong swimmer, and he has two legs."

"Jesus!" says Sharon, she's come up on them somehow without Rowena noticing. "Jesus, Mom! Is this all really necessary?" And then she's stomping off, kicking pieces of oyster shell out of her way, marching to the other end of the cemetery again. Rowena watches her go, not sure what she should do here. There's a certain ritual at work, she's pretty sure, but she has no idea what her role is.

Sharon's mom rustles in her purse. Rowena is watching her now, staring at her in a way that would seem rude in other circumstances. Here, suddenly, rules like that no longer apply.

She pulls out not a Kleenex like you'd expect, but a chocolate bar, an Oh Henry! in its bright yellow wrapper. She holds it in two hands and then snaps it in half, still in its wrapper. She hands half to Rowena. "Oh He" the piece says, and Rowena does her best not to see any significance in this.

"Thank you," says Rowena.

"You're welcome," says Sharon's mom. And then they both turn back to stare again at the leg, chewing together in silence.

Sharon is still off at the far end of the cemetery, furiously smoking another cigarette. She tosses her head, flicking it from side to side, making a large point of not looking in their direction. Rowena has no idea what is making her so angry, but she figures that it's her business and no-one else's. She's starting to think that Sharon doesn't really need a reason, or not a very big one, anyway.

Rowena mulls this over as she finishes her chocolate bar, which is very good. She licks her fingers and then hands the empty wrapper to Sharon's mom, who has held her hand out for it. Sharon's mom crumples the two half-wrappers up into a ball and tucks them back in her purse. All the while they've been staring at the leg, at the stone, in the ghostly direction of Lloyd, gone but definitely not forgotten.

Sharon's mom turns now and stares off in the other direction. Rowena turns too and sees that from where they're standing there really is a view. Through the trees there is a clear patch of sky and outlined against that, far in the distance, is a mountain range and the white smudge of a glacier. "That's beautiful," Rowena says.

"Sharon tells me you were married," Sharon's mom says.

"Yes, I was," Rowena says.

"What happened?"

Jesus, what happened? An earthquake happened, a tidal wave, locusts and poisonous toads fell from the sky. "I don't know," Rowena says. "He left. It was over, I guess." She thinks about it, as if she hadn't considered it before. For some reason she wants to do right by this woman. "I don't know."

Sharon's mom nods, still staring at the glacier, not looking at Rowena. Rowena looks at her, though, and thinks for the second time that this is a nice-looking woman, a friendly, nice woman.

"Why do you do this?" Rowena asks.

"This?"

"Come here, bring the leg, all of it. Sharon thinks that you believe he'll come back. That somehow he'll return to get his leg. Is that what you believe?"

Sharon's mom is perfectly still. She doesn't say anything for a second and then, "No," she says, "I don't believe that."

Rowena can't leave it alone. "Then why? Why do you do it?"

Sharon's mom turns now and looks at her. "Because it helps," she says.

Sharon is waiting for them. They pack up the leg, load the car and are off in less than two minutes. Driving away, Rowena hopes that she gets to do this again next year. She'd like that, she thinks, that is something she'd really like to do.

Runs Good, Some Rust

My husband left me, for reasons I don't want to get into right now, and he took my car. He took a lot of other things as well, but when he drove off—a puff of blue smoke into the sunset—it was in my car.

I bought it new in 1972, a white Plymouth Valiant, and it was the only car I'd ever owned. I bought it because of the name.

People, men, would come up to me over the years and want to talk about Valiants. They'd talk about slant sixes and threes in the tree, and the old days with push-button automatics in the dashboard. I was polite to them, I'm polite to everybody—I'm polite to the cat, I'm polite to the *refrigerator*—but they couldn't understand. I wasn't interested in Valiants or their transmissions or their six cylinders, slanted or otherwise. I loved my car because it was mine—we'd grown into each other. I wasn't interested in anyone else's.

Now, though, I needed a new car. And if I couldn't have mine back, I'd get another just like her—or as close as I could manage. It's easier to readjust this way.

So, when I saw the ad in the classifieds I took it as a sign. '72 brown Valiant. Runs good, some rust. 871-7979.'

I phoned and the phone rang six times before it was picked up. "Yes?" said a man's voice. It didn't sound like a voice that would describe a car as running 'good' but you never know. Perhaps the copy person in the advertisement department was the one. I didn't want to buy a car that ran 'good.' Such a thing wouldn't affect its slant six or its whatever, but it would be a dirty little secret that I'd promise to forget and never would.

"Yes?" said the man again. And in not many more words than it takes to tell it, I arranged to come and see his car. It's a funny thing that we, I mean I, will trust a stranger if only we have a context to do it in. I won't accept rides from male coworkers, men I've worked with for ten years, but I will take a taxi to a strange man's home because that is what you do. I find this odd myself, but there you go.

The house sat in the middle of a yard that consisted of lawn, nothing more. A concrete sidewalk led up to the front door, which was between two windows. The roof was black. It was the most nondescript house I'd ever seen. Even a child's drawing of a house would have a cat in the window, or a smoking chimney sticking out of the top.

It had an aluminum screen door and I rapped on that. Its ridges hurt my knuckles and, though it rattled noisily, I doubt any sound whatsoever carried within the house. I rapped again, and then opened the screen to knock on the inner door. This one was thickly varnished wood and I had to knock three times, waiting each time, before I heard footsteps.

The door opened and the man stood there, holding his door while I held mine. "Hello," I said, but he stared at me. "I've come about the car for sale?" I said stupidly, turning the statement into a question. "I phoned a little while ago?"

He nodded, and stepped forward. "It's around back," he said, closing his door behind him. What could I do but follow?

The backyard was another stretch of grass. A short asphalt driveway cut it in two. Two new-looking galvanized garbage containers sat next to the driveway, the only things in the yard. The street address was stencilled on them in white paint. The grass was so perfect it looked manufactured.

His car was parked in the driveway and, while identical to mine, looked nothing like her. I could have walked across some invisible line back into 1972. This car still had its hubcaps. The paint was not just intact, it shone. Here and there, in the seams of the metal, I could see tiny blobs of wax. I saw no rust. I felt slightly nervous at the prospect of owning such an immaculate car.

The man stood beside the car. He didn't lean on the car, or

cross his arms, or bend one leg—he stood. Until I saw him like that I hadn't realized how nobody stands this way. I pictured him driving this car: sitting erect, both hands on the wheel, two miles per hour beneath the speed limit.

He gestured toward the car. "Try it," he said, and held out the keys, two of them on a ring attached to a worn leather fob. "Take it for a drive."

Neither of us moved for a second. Then I took the keys, opened the door and got in.

I started the engine and sat for a few seconds, waiting for the man to say something, anything, through the open window. Finally I put the lever into 'reverse' and backed down the short driveway. "I'll be right back," I called, and he nodded.

I pulled over a few blocks later and just sat, leaving the engine running. The car wasn't as new-looking as I had first thought, just worn in places I didn't expect. Unlike Valerie, unlike my old Valiant, the vinyl of the bench seat wasn't cracked. A depression was worn in the seat, though, the vinyl faded and the stuffing of the seat compressed where he must have sat. This depression wasn't quite where I was used to sitting, but was too far over toward the centre of the car, so that I sat half in and half out of it.

The dashboard, too, was intact, though it also was worn, as if the man rubbed it with his hand as he drove. The sun visor on the driver's side was ripped and then repaired with scotch tape that had turned yellow and brittle. The glove compartment held nothing but the owner's manual, a book I must have owned but could not remember ever having seen.

It didn't smell like my car.

When I returned the man wasn't in the yard. I sat in the car for a few moments, waiting, and then I shut the engine off and got out. I walked up to the back door and knocked. I knocked again and the man opened the door. He looked down at me, but he didn't say anything. I opened my mouth, closed it, and then opened it again.

"The car is fine," I said. "How much do you want for it?"

"You take it home and drive it for a few days. Then pay me what you think it's worth. Take a week," he said.

I started to say something, but the door was already closing.

"He did what?" asked my friend Ruby. By then I'd gotten used to the idea, even thought it was somehow appropriate or reasonable. Ruby almost coughed her coffee back through her nose. Sometimes I marvel that Ruby and I exist in the same world. Ruby seems connected to thoughts and emotions that are completely alien to me. She's my oldest friend.

"He doesn't know your name?" I shook my head. "Or where you live?" I sipped my coffee and shook my head again. "Jeeeesus," said Ruby. She stood up. Ruby drives a city bus and works a split shift, so she has time to meet me in the early afternoon for lunch or coffee, or whatever. I'm an accountant. Actually I'm not quite an accountant, I'm a bookkeeper, but I do everything that an accountant does, though for a lot less money, so I've promoted myself. At least to myself.

"Is he cute, at least?" Ruby asked as we left the coffee shop. "Who knows, maybe he's..."

"I'll pay more attention next time," I said.

I parked out front. The car was mine, now, so I didn't think it would be proper to park it in his driveway. I knocked on the wooden door and waited to hear footsteps. Did the house have a basement? What took him so long? The door finally opened and he stood there, dressed as before, looking at me.

"Hi," I said, "it's me." He nodded. "I've come to pay you for the car. It runs very well." He nodded again, holding the door open with his right hand. I took out my cheque-book and pen and began filling out a cheque, balancing my purse in the crook of my left arm as a desk. He didn't ask me to come in.

"I don't know your name," I said.

"Oh," he said, and looked down at the cheque and then at

me. "I see," he said, and told me, spelling it out for me though it was a very plain name.

"There you go," I said, and handed him the cheque. "Thanks again. I think I'm going to like the car." I let go of the screen door and walked back along the sidewalk.

I heard the screen door open. "You haven't filled in the cheque," he called. "You've signed it, but the amount is blank."

By now I was standing in the street, the car between me and the man. "I know," I said. "I thought I'd leave it to you to fill in whatever you think it's worth." I opened the driver's door, waved, and then sat down. I could see him in the rear-view mirror, watching me as I drove away.

A month passed. I didn't hear from him, though I suppose I didn't really expect to. Still, my name and address were on the cheque. And he didn't cash the cheque, either. I'd go to the bank each week to update my account book, driving there in a car that still didn't feel like mine, curious to see how much I had paid for it, and still the cheque hadn't been cashed.

"Maybe he lost it," said Ruby. "Maybe he's some kind of crazy philanthropist with a fleet of '72 Valiants that he gives to needy women." We were having lunch, me in my 'accountant's drag' as Ruby calls it: a skirt and jacket combination with black pumps. She in her bus uniform, of course: grey pants with a blue uniform jacket covered in various patches and union pins. Part of our friendship, I think, is that we each privately regard the other as ridiculous. "Maybe he's like Elvis with his Cadillacs or whatever." Ruby is very strong-minded. Once she gets onto a topic there is little one can do to get her off.

"Phone him," she said. "Better yet, drop by. What the hell, take a chance. This guy could turn out to be Prince Charming." She toyed with her coffee cup, something she does a lot of since she quit smoking. "Who knows, maybe you'll start a fire or something, this guy might—"

"I'll think about it," I said.

I'd go for drives sometimes. I was still getting to know the car, and it helped. I like to be by myself, and I enjoy the scenery, so why not? Sometimes I'd drive for hours, go on actual trips on the highway to some place and then turn right around and come home. It was the driving I liked, not the destination.

I'd daydream. I'd wonder what it would be like, riding along with him driving. Maybe I'd cuddle up close, like you see teenagers do. Maybe I did it too, when I was younger. I don't remember. Maybe we'd park somewhere to watch the sunset. Both of us looking out the window, not saying a word. He'd rest his hand on my neck, just where it meets my shoulder. His hand would be cool. He'd slide his hand down the top of my blouse while we both looked straight ahead, sliding his fingers down underneath my brassière so that when my nipple became erect it would push between his first and second fingers. Neither of us would say a word as we watched the last light of the sun bend up at us from beneath the world.

Or we could be driving along the same highway that I take on my trips. Him steering with his left hand, resting his right hand on my knee, but staring intently through the windshield because he was driving so fast. I'd watch the trees flash by one after another as, so slowly as to be almost imaginary, his hand would float up my left thigh. It would flutter underneath my skirt, his palm warm and cold against my skin.

I'd drive along, my hands at the ten and two o'clock position on the steering-wheel, heading home.

Ruby came to my apartment for dinner and told me that she'd been fired. "Well, not fired exactly. Given a six-month suspension." She poured us each another glass of wine. She'd brought a bottle of cheap Italian red, the only wine she drank, and one that I was beginning to appreciate as well. Ruby says it's the only wine you can buy that tastes like it has been made by somebody, somewhere. It might not be good, but you think of somebody's grandfather while you drink it.

"My god, Ruby, what happened? What did you do?" Ruby was fully capable of anything, I knew that.

"Well," she said, "I think it's time for me to take a rest, anyway. If I don't take some time off I'll probably wind up killing somebody." She took a drink of wine. "It gets to you, after a while. People at you all the time, in your face for no reason other than the fact that you're there for them, a target."

"And?"

"And I guess this guy was the last straw."

I nodded. "And?"

"So finally I stopped the bus and told him to get off. Which he does. But then he leans back in and starts again, his head sticking way out on his neck, you know?"

I nodded, wondering what was coming next.

"And so I closed the doors and drove off."

"While the guy was—"

"Yeah, his head was still in the door and he was running sideways down the sidewalk, screaming. Oh, I was real mad." She paused. "I pulled the bus over, let him go and phoned dispatch. I told them, 'Get someone else to drive this bus. I'm finished.'" She took another drink of wine. "Oh, I was mad."

I laughed, picturing Ruby. I sat there, chuckling, and she watched me, amused that I found it funny.

I put a pot of perfume in the car. They have those now, perfume for cars. I'd had one in Valerie, and before that a succession of those green Christmas Tree things that never quite manage to smell like a pine forest. I still felt like I was sitting half-in and half-out of the seat, but it was getting better. It takes a long time to feel comfortable, I believe. A process has to take place, a slow wearing together. I don't know if other people are as sensitive to this as I am.

I let two more weeks go by. I even drove by his house once, telling myself that it was on the way from somewhere to somewhere else, but I didn't see him. The curtains were open, showing a front room that could have been a display of prizes for a tv game show. The cheque still hadn't been cashed.

Finally I took Ruby with me. We drove over to his house and parked out front. "Nice house," Ruby said, rolling her eyes. "Very...orderly." We walked up the path and Ruby stood there while I opened the screen door and knocked. No-one answered. Ruby didn't notice but when we were driving away I thought I saw the curtains rustle.

I went to my bank and opened another account. I transferred all of my money into the new account, leaving only 800 dollars. That night I drove to his house and pulled up in back, driving right up his driveway. I sat there for a long time, the engine running and the headlights shining on the wall and windows of the house. Finally I put the car in reverse and backed away. Driving home I settled down into the seat, feeling comfortable, feeling like everything was all right.

KELLEY AITKEN

A la Playa

At the beach you hardly ever bathe. Clarify this, you hardly ever wash. The hype of hygiene, your North American fastidiousness, hasn't survived the journey to the Andes or this side-trip to the coast. But daily, you enter the ocean, admitting to only one of your companions, the man who loves you, that it makes you nervous—the sea, huge and relentless and rendered again and again upon the sand. There is no real danger of drowning, but you only frolic when he is with you.

You can picture this from a bird's-eye view. A pair of heads, two sets of shoulders, his more deeply tanned than yours. The artist in you, storing the image for further use, notes: true to the conventions of Egyptian tomb painting—he/dark, she/light. Four arms like noodles out over the fat shiny tire, bobbing on an immensity of sparkling, swelling green. Beneath the surface, shadowy wiggles, four legs like tentacles drooping from the big black octopus head.

Toes touching his and then sand, drifting toward beach, toward rocks, one foot glancing off of, oooo-what-is-it, something weird and woolly. Snaps you back into the tube and out of your airborne vision, dumps your consciousness into the immediate. He grunts. You produce a little shriek.

In a few minutes the two of you will haul it up the beach, an old net in the shape of a body, you'll pull out the coral snagged in the folds, the shells and jagged cups of barnacle, chewed-up cork, hooks, and here or there a knotted mass of line, all of it complicated and compacted into this thing that weighs as much or more than a drowned sailor, and the excitement and mystery of it will fade when it proves itself to be nothing more than a drowned net.

After the dip you rinse off in brackish water from the shower-head attached to your host's house. The water gouts and sputters and then leers out of a plastic clown face screwed to mouldy cement. Some days you soap up but the ungainly squat and your hand shovelling at the crotch of your suit; the fact that everybody smells the same, of sweat and tanning lotion and bug cream and beer; and sometimes just the weird red grin leering at you from around the shower nozzle, makes you hold back from being too scrupulous in your ablutions. Instead you let the water decide, running down over your head and shoulders. You snap the sleek black tanksuit away from your cleavage, once, twice. You can't really be bothered getting cleaner than this.

The man loves you but you won't fuck. He won't try and you won't invite. You'll share a bed and snuggle a bit, until with a sigh you say, "Too hot," and push him away. But you're at the beach, so you think about sex a lot, it's accumulating in layers like the creams and lotions on your skin, like the slightly greasy feel of sea air, another epidermis, laid on and glued down by wind.

You find the toucan head on the first day, walking alone toward Tonchigue, the fishing village a mile south of where you stay. It's strange, a red and yellow and green hook of a thing, hanging just out of reach on a dried stalk, reed-like, part of a parched bush backed up against a cliff. You throw pebbles and shells at it before you know what it is, trying to shake it loose from its perch. Finally you go in search of a stick and flip what you now recognize as a beak over your head. You wonder where the bird died, not here, higher probably; and this, the part the vultures didn't want, was dropped and where it snagged and stuck the only things to find it were the ants that have picked it almost clean. The lower beak hangs slack, bleached, still attached but tenuously, by black cords of sinew or skin. The skull is perfect, smooth on top and at the sides.

Only underneath are there scraps of leathery flesh. One round dried marble of an eyeball clicks against the beak. It stinks. You carry it back to the house, wondering what invisible form of lice might now be travelling from dead bird to live woman, setting up shop on sunburnt skin, crawling through the forest of fine blond hairs on a forearm. You perch the skull on the sharpened cane fence of your host's house. It presides over the visit, a bird god. Sightless, silent, beaky.

Later that night you are at the beach-side bar run by the balding Italian with the lisp, whose body is firm and muscular, whose balls bulge in a skimpy thong underneath his designer t-shirt. He rescues his pet spider monkey from a clutch of taunting squealing children on the balcony. The monkey is squealing too. The Italian brings it on its string leash to where you are half-seated, half-splayed-out, an awkward position dictated by the mad mechanics of the wooden deck chair into which you melted after too much lobster and too many beers. He introduces the monkey to your lap as if the two might be made for each other, at least the monkey thinks so, and the man, as an afterthought, looks at your face and queries, "*Te molesta?*"

You have never had a monkey in your lap before and you are wondering what kind of lice or fleas or tics or chiggers are housed in its short sleek fur or alternatively what kind of disease you will contract if it bites you, what about that AIDS theory, the thoughts spin and shuck and drop in your mind like tumblers on Lottario day and you decide, never mind, death by tropical infection or infestation, and you say, "*No, no me moleste,*" because the feel of the monkey in your lap and its delicate fingers on your arm and its dear bleached scalp are worth the thousand terrors that have somersaulted through your consciousness in the last ten seconds. It's like a baby. You want a baby. But on a balmy night beside the ocean, just north of the equator, on a night when no baby has yet appeared, miraculous, in your womb, you discover that a spider monkey, temporarily, will do.

At the beach you hardly ever bathe. You dip in and out of salt water and salt air and accumulate layers. Of fish juice and the cold drips running down beer bottles onto your skirt, bug repellent, sun lotion, the squeeze of lemon over *cebiche*, the shrimp guts and squid ink that paint your palms and finger-nails and arms and legs. You are becoming biosphere and the ocean breeze circles you like a testimony, like a story of your new and ancient self.

You always feel like this on the beach, naked and yet not, solid and yet permeable. Usually horny as hell. Wet sand under-foot—you can't get enough walking—you want to walk the coastal length of this continent but you turn back before Tonchigue, you turn back at the pier, iced like a cake with frigates and vultures and pelicans, the memory of its attach-ment to land hanging still in the emptiness between it and the shore. Dozens of birds. The white throat-sacks of the frigates, the yawn and stretch of an occasional pelican shaking its pouch for a snack, the preternatural brood of vultures hulking higher up on the abandoned shed at the end of the pier.

You hardly ever bathe at the beach because there's a metal trunk in the shower stall of the one bathroom and the toilet is lined in grime and salt rime and always smells like someone just took a dump. For the first few days you are not aware of the other bathroom, ensuite to the master bedroom. You have already postulated that your host has adopted the habit of "doing a growler"—this is the language your friends use—in the ocean. You know most men in this country pee on bushes and hedges and fences and walls and tires or on nothing but the baked brown dirt out behind houses. By the time you discover that this other bathroom exists, with its relatively clean and private tub, you have resigned yourself to the salt and fish stink of your skin. The knowledge of this extra bath-room is a luxury item in the file of your brain. You categorize it under non-necessities.

One day it rains and you stand under it, letting it slick down your body. The man who loves you wants to help you wash. He hasn't seen your breasts in seven years or your bare ass in twelve. You were lovers once, that long ago, and for nostalgia or something less definable you shared a bed the last time you visited this strange and wonderful country, but he was still married and so you kept your panties on and now time has solidified the feelings between you but the motions are more difficult. He pours buckets of rainwater over your head. You use shampoo. Your body feels babe-like and rubbery. You say to yourself that you're washing off years. The palm fronds drip all afternoon. The man who loves you makes lazy proposals of marriage that involve varying increments of weight loss for him and waiting for you. All day long, he plans a fish chow-der. You help him by looking in a stained and tattered cook-book whose backcover and several pages are missing. From "D" onwards the index is gone. You settle for bouillabaisse. The flies thicken the soupy air inside the house. Fish heads bubble on the stove. One eyeball floats to the surface, opaque as a cataract. You think of Innu children but can't bring your-self to snack on the proffered delicacy.

You force the man who loves you to "talk turkey" about his plans. You are relentless, insistent as a dentist's drill. He keeps reaching for *The Joy of Cooking* as a way of changing the subject, an ineffectual detour from the single track you're on, fish soup be damned. You alternate tough questions with your own assessment of his life so far. You cite examples of older expa-triate drunks. "Don't end up like them," you say. His eyes are hurt behind the polaroid lenses of his glasses when he responds, "You think I haven't thought of it?"

The next day you're swinging lazy in the hammock in the red light of late afternoon. He stands over you and, with his thigh, stops you mid-sway. Leaning over the hammock, he says, "You're in danger of becoming a bitch," and pauses. Then, taking courage from your silence, he goes on, "Because you're so opinionated."

You resist the urge to fight back. He has a point. You could argue his choice of words but not his right to say this from out of the vulnerable part of him you exposed yesterday like a surgeon. You know you are like a drug to him and that he doesn't yet know how much he can take, neither the allowable dosage nor the frequency. He is at sea in you. He is a little boat tossed about on your waves and you are the great devouring saltwater womb. You don't mean to be but that's not the issue. Whatever you do keeps tossing him high in spray-filled air and flinging him down on a drum-hard beach. Bitch.

His body has aged outward, flesh hanging heavy on his medium build. His hair has developed that indeterminate colour exhibited by men in their fifties. He is regrowing the moustache he had for over twenty years that the Ecuadorian girlfriend convinced him to shave off. He is deeply tanned and weathered and uses his body well, which makes the girth of him bearable to you who are so vain about appearances. You tease him about his gut. His toes and ankles are those of a fisherman, gnarled and choked with varicose veins. A great scar like a sickle embraces him under his ribs, a chunk of liver gone, delivered finally onto an operating table after years of recurrent malaria made worse by drink.

He's done his share of drugs too. Cocaine for the most part. He's separated from the wife who has not stopped huddling over the smoking screen, who is enticed back ad nauseum to the sweet sickly stink of base and all that it fitfully promises. He thinks of you as the love of his life but you know you've

85

only earned the title by default. The part of you that isn't a bitch worries that you've pared him down too much, too close to the bone. But instead you say, "I was worried that I was just a symbol to you." This, after his prediction of your impending status as the kind of woman men avoid. He is stunned. Hurt.

"Symbol of what?"

You don't say it but you think it—the light princess. Sunshine, laughter. All that she isn't, now. Snow White or Cinderella compared to his wife, a burnt-out Dragon Queen. You remember just in time that everyone is human. Even you. He has treated you with gentle humour and affection all week. You wonder what it is about softness in a man that brings out the talons in you and at the same time this icy shield. You love him too, in a way that you can never admit, because the pity part of it may be for something in yourself. That after all these years, this is the marriage you are offered, the pairing, perhaps, that you deserve.

You acquiesce enough each night to kiss him goodnight before you turn to sleep on your side at the edge of the bed facing the door. Knowing that in your dreams, you'll veer toward the symbolic, wanting to be sure of an escape route. You poke him when he snores. He does with regularity. In the morning you ask if you snored too. "Gently," he says, "I could hardly hear it." He goes on, "It's sweet." And more, "kinda sexy."

You have to admit you love the way he loves you. No demands. You don't know if you could have sex with him anymore. A rhetorical question. It strikes you that it would be easy to marry him. That maybe sex leaves so many marriages because it's the volatile component, the need and heat. You can imagine yourself growing old with him, trading off more and more of the gender roles. He loves to cook and doesn't mind cleaning. You tell him he'll have to teach you how to take apart the engine of his Harley. You like this man. He is as calm as a rock, as rooted as a tree and only windblown where you're concerned. You love the way he treats you, moving around your perimeter with gentle wariness, with solid affection. When he takes you to the bus in Esmeraldas, the one that will take you away from him, he reaches for your hand as you cross the street.

Holding hands with him is the most comfortable place you've been in eight years. You do not tell him this. You board the bus after wriggling out of his sweaty grasp. You are going to miss him like mad.

You wash the beach off you as soon as you arrive back in the city. You stand for half an hour under hot water. You knead your scalp and suds your armpits, you scrub at the unrealized potential of him between your legs. You wash it all away, the need, the possibility, the kindness of him, the sweaty fish stinkiness of sea. You rinse clear of the past and the future. Sand swirls in the tub and down the drain. You step out.

Nickname

She's walking by the hen house when she hears, from inside, sounds of a commotion. Is it a *zorro*? She's lost chickens this way before, to an animal that looks like a fox. Shit. And no stick to bang on the outside of the henhouse. No worker around to help her out. But my chickens, she thinks, I have to do something. And just as it dawns on her that a *zorro* is nocturnal and wouldn't be hunting in the middle of the day, she finds herself reacting in panic. A man. Coming out of the doorway. Cortita's son?! Stumbling out of the dusty, acrid gloom, one hand on his zipper, the other held up as if to ward off a blow.

The way I heard it first, the way she told it—she had no idea what was going on. What she'd interrupted. Not until she was down at the dock and the men—embarrassed and amused—spelled it out for her. But that's getting ahead of her tale. And Nicky is so good at telling stories.

Cortita's son—whose name I learned but promptly forgot, remembering only the nickname that attached itself to him after the incident—scrambling like an animal pursued out of its warren. He's running now, slipping down the hill behind the stout stilts of the large cane house, finally crashing into the bush at the base of the slope. Sounds of his crazy progress drift up to Nicky long after she's lost sight of him, staring stunned at the two deep gouges he's carved into the hill, skid marks of his mad descent.

She enters the small *cana* shed, waits for her eyes to adjust. The hens are fussing, clucking, pecking at each other. One of them isn't moving. Is, in fact, dead; still warm but disembowelled after a fashion, pink entrails protruding from under its tail. She panics. Grabs the dead hen and runs, not in the direction taken by the fleeing man but down the south slope of the hill to the path that leads along the dikes surrounding the shrimp ponds to the loading dock. Her husband is working with two friends, a Brit and an American. They are fixing one of the boat motors. She is in a state, breathless and gasping, tears streaming down her face, when she arrives at the cement dock.

"My best hen," she blurts out, crying in earnest now, like a baby, great gulps of air punctuating her speech, "my hen, my best hen."

The chicken's legs dangle uselessly, its head flopping to the side, one tiny eye open and glazed, gazing heavenward, and the other—as if conspiratorial in its own demise—closed, a final wink. The men begin to laugh, reading between the lines; one of them throws back his head and crows. The hen's neck is a rubbery tube in Nicky's fist, pink organs bounce as she brandishes the bird at her friends, whose response bewilders her. She is near hysteria. Small arcs of blood spray onto the cement.

Nicky doesn't know yet. She doesn't know that if you ring a chicken's neck, spasms and contractions will twist throughout its intestinal system as it dies. Providing stimulation to anything inside the chicken. She doesn't know and so she is inadvertently playing this absurd game of show and tell. Showing her dead hen to the men, who know that it's a case of bestiality. The men know, and cannot help their laughter, are amused even as Nicky slumps to the ground, tears streaming from her red nose onto her crossed rubber boots. She's cradling the hen, staring at it, when the puzzle of its body is explained by the Brit, confirmed by the American, and the sound from her mouth, her hand flying up to stifle it, is the horror of finally understanding. It wipes the embarrassed smiles off the men's faces. Her husband bends down to her, gently pries the bird loose from her grip, offers his arm. She leans on him heavily all the way back up to the house.

He pours her a strong drink. Leads her to the hammock on the verandah, kisses her wet cheek, picks the dead bird up from the railing where he laid it when they opened the cane gate of the porch and, walking around behind the house, starts down the hill.

Later that evening, over rum watered with more tears, Nicky laments the loss. The pain suffered by the bird, and hers, imagining its death, is what she buries first—so many years in this country, without a hard edge, you don't survive. It's easier to focus on the unlaid eggs; the hen was her most productive, her "best." And there's the meal they will not have. Any other bird dying in this yard would end up in the pot, chicken a rare treat in the steady diet of shrimp. But not this one. "That fucker," she says. Then, in spite of crying and due to the fourth rum before her on the table, when it might be observed that she is rather enjoying the drama of it all, Nicky giggles and says, "That chicken-fucker." And so Cortita's son becomes known as The Chicken Fucker.

I meet him almost a year after the event, when he helps to push the boat out one sun-saturated morning, along the deep muddy channel that connects the shrimp farm to the river. I'm down for a visit from my job in Quito, teaching English as a foreign language.

It's Thanksgiving, there are six of us going on a picnic to an island farther south. We'll head for town first to pick up beer, cheese and bread. *Queso. Cervesas.* It's already noon and we're impatient but there's not enough tide yet to float the boat to the spot where the channel floor drops away. We're sinking knee-deep in mud trying to manoeuvre the Boston whaler toward the bay. It's slow going. The mood is souring.

The smiling youth appears out of the mangrove alongside the channel and calls out *saludos* to the group. He offers to help, lays down his machete, steps neatly out of his boots, rolls his pants above the knee and hops into the thick mud. In English I ask, "Who is this?" Someone whispers a reply. "Who?!" Shocked. "Shh, we'll tell you later."

He's got the compact musculature typical of the area. Ropey arms, small hips. Broad features in an almost ugly face. Lives with his mother, the tiny woman affectionately named Cortita, in a little cane house in the rainforest behind the shrimp farm. Father unknown and long gone. They are one of the poorest families around and with the exception of this man's sister—pretty Bibiana with her own fatherless family—illiterate. Cortita knows the saints days of the calendar year, rattles off seven saints for any given week, lists a month of saints at a time and only stalls twice in a recitation of the annual list, 365 saints, *Gracias a Dios*. She knows the secrets of the woods as well, which leaf to press to a fevered forehead, which bark to brew for coughs, this dried plant mixed with the yolk of a day-old egg for rheumatism, this one burned in the four corners of a house to rid it of unwanted ghosts. The boy should marry soon but won't. Some say he's slow, "not all there." He was the last of her children, born after she thought her womb had given up. Even before the incident, she'd shake her head when she mentioned his name.

Within minutes we've pushed the boat to the right spot. The story is saved until after our full-out sprint across the bay, until after the boat is anchored, the cooler of beer buried in the wet sand at the wave edge and we're sitting in the tepid shallows on our picnic island.

Nicky unwinds her tale like a *maestro*, the narrative fuelled by brief interjections from her husband Dan, who has stationed himself further up the slope of beach and is now layering sand by the wet handful over his outstretched legs. The others have wandered off, collecting shells, they've heard this one before. "You tell the rest," she says, when she's reached the point of her collapse into the swinging hammock. I'm disbelieving, imagination struggling against propriety.

Over and over my mind reverses to the beginning, filling in the parts that Nicky couldn't see or know. It's an insistent film, playing itself out: Cortita's son in the chicken shed, his body and hands in shadow, the chickens squawking, footsteps through the grass, his face turning toward the avenue of sunshine from the shed's doorway, his actions blurred and manic when he realizes someone is outside, the wild explosion of his escape out of the tiny shed. I see him running until he reaches the safety of the forest and running still, slipping and sliding down the bush-festooned slope, swinging by one cupped hand round a fruit-bearing tree, a sweet fug in his nostrils from the overripe and fallen fruits beneath his feet. One leap across the river to the smooth washing stone at its centre, another to the opposite bank, up the slick clay path to a way between the trees that even now, in the beginning of the dry season, needs to be cleared of creepers daily. Running until he sees the tiny cane house, the oil drum at its corner that catches runoff from the roof, right through the tiny clearing where Cortita's hens stoop and pick and now scatter in a screech at his drumming feet, into the bush again until he stops, gasping, lungs pounding and collapses against a tree, adrenalin draining away painfully. He stares unseeing back at the house, back in the direction he came from.

Where Cortita finds him, minutes later, on her return from foraging for nightshade. He does not tell her what is wrong, only that, by now, he realizes his machete is not with him, is instead where he put it down, just inside the entrance to the chicken shed. Cortita stares at her son, who in turn is staring straight ahead through the thicket of bushes at nothing, at his own fear perhaps, or at a scene playing and replaying behind his eyes. She cuffs him once on the back of the head, not too hard, walks through the clearing into her house, lays the plant she's found on the tiny wooden table, touches the cross at her neck and heads down the path toward the shrimp farm.

"I met her at the river," says Nicky's husband Dan, picking up the story, "She was coming to get his machete.

"Well you know Cortita. She greeted me and asked about my health and Nicky's health. I said we were both fine—well, Nicky's upset—I said. I was starting to feel nervous, I mean, I really had no plan when I started down to their house, I was mad I suppose, determined to teach him a lesson. Maybe I was going to make him pay for the chicken, penalize him in some way, tell him he couldn't work at the farm for a while, I don't know." Dan sounds perplexed even now, responding all over again to a situation he would have preferred to avoid.

"I hadn't even thought about Cortita," he continues, "and there she was in front of me on the path, this little old woman who's done so much for us. I had the hen in my hand, was holding it like this," he gestures with his right hand off to the side, a sheepish look on his face. "I think I said his name, her son's name, and then, I didn't know what to do, I was just holding the dead bird and standing there like an idiot.

"She stared at it for a while and then I said she could get the machete. We both knew where he'd left it." He pauses in his story and for a moment surveys the sand landscape he has built around his legs. "She reached out her hand for the chicken and laid it gently on the ground without looking at me.

"I muttered something, I don't remember what. She hadn't looked at me this whole time. Then I said—look, I'll get the machete, you wait here—and she said no, she needed to see the

Senora, to make her apologies. I said—oh Cortita, it's not your fault!—I mean, we still hadn't, you know, talked about the way the hen died." He pauses, mired in euphemism. All the while he's clawing at the beach, his fists closing around clumps of wet sand at his side.

"Anyways," he continues, "she gave me this look, fierce, kind of, or proud and she said—he's my son—and then she shook her head, the way she always did," he pauses, and it could be that he's remembering that moment, the prick of sweat at his collar, his discomfort. "She led the way back up to the house."

"All she said to me," Nicky speaks up, "was—*nunca*, Senora, *nunca*, this will never happen again—and then she said she would pay for the hen. I started to protest, I mean, Cortita has no money, no work except what she occasionally does for us. She wouldn't be talked out of it, though."

She glances over her shoulder at her husband, his legs still encased in sand. "You're right, she looked so, mmm, powerful. Determined. And then she got the machete and went back home."

"We don't know what she did with the chicken," Dan pauses. "It wasn't something we could ask about."

"Cortita's done some wild things to people," Nicky laughs, "I figure anything's possible. Maybe she nailed the hen to his bed while it rotted, or smeared parts of it on his pillow and let him live with it for a while. No, that would mean she'd have to live with it too, the stink of it in the house." Unlike Dan, Nicky is savouring the tale, showing it off. "Oh I know, I bet you she cooked it. Made him eat it—the whole thing. Yuck."

"Anyways, she came to the house every day for a month after that and cleaned and cooked for us and wouldn't take any money and finally I just said—Cortita, you've paid for the hen!—and she said, no Senora, not yet, but I could tell she was tired. Before this she'd only worked two or three days a week for us.

"Gradually, she let us start paying her again." Nicky smacks at a sand flea on her arm. "When she let us give her a small bucket of shrimp, I figured it was over. We didn't see The Chicken Fucker for three months at least, did we, honey?"

Dan sighs. "Nope," he replies. Heaving himself out of his sand bed, he stands upright and brushes the grit from his thighs and shins. As he walks toward the water, pellets of sand dislodge themselves from his creased shorts. They bounce lightly on the beach. He wades in up to his waist and then dives.

Nicky's eyes are closed now, head tilted back, face bare to the sun. We sit in silence for several minutes. I'm watching Dan. He's way out, a small brown dot swimming through a field of silver. Nicky stirs, takes a last sip of the beer that she's canted into the sand at her side. "Whadya say," she winks at me, a raconteur delighted by her own punchline, "chicken for dinner?"

I don't see Dan and Nicky for a long time. At Easter, one of my students offers me a ride to the coast. I shed layers all the way down the mountain, stuffing first jacket, then sweater, then socks into my duffel bag as we descend into green soupy heat. I lean my head out the window as we come into Muisne, smiling at the barefoot kids who run, for a while, beside the car. It's sunset, too late to go anywhere. I stay overnight and arrange for a boat to the farm in the morning.

The *canoa* drops me at the far edge of the property. I sink halfway up my shins in the stinking mud. The tide is still out.

Nicky waves from the packing area, shouts something I can't hear. She turns to dispatch a worker, someone to carry my bag and help me through the mud.

There's an art to this but it's one I've never mastered. I've seen women in pretty dresses and shiny black pumps walk a gang-plank from a crowded ship to a muddy bank, slip off their shoes and pick their way daintily to a higher, drier spot. They don't hesitate or, miracle of miracles, get dirty.

Not a speck of the slippery grey muck on their full cotton skirts or slim brown legs. I feel huge and North American, stranded in the mud in my rubber thongs, afraid to venture from this perch, the twin mud pits in which my feet are mired, captive. Nothing to do but wait. The men in the *canoa* bid me a laughing farewell. The worker is on his way. He's got a pair of rubber boots in one hand.

It's The Chicken Fucker. And so this makes the second time he has come to my aid, striding gracefully through the mud. He greets me. Tactful, polite. I have to lean on his arm to rinse my feet in the channel before putting on the boots. He carries my bag slung over one shoulder as if it weighed no more than a feather pillow. He offers the other arm as support. We move slowly, aiming toward the distant loading dock where Nicky and Dan and a handful of their workers are going about their daily business. My hands are sweaty, already smeared with mud. The skin of his arm is smooth and firm. I know the sensa-tions running rampant in my body. I know the lick of lust that grips me when he turns to lift me over a fallen tree in our path, hanging my bag on one of its branches momentarily so that he has both arms free to carry me over the log. I know he feels none of this, is simply doing his job, helping the clumsy visit-ing gringa. There is a slope now and he heads down first, posi-tioning his body so that I can slip down after him, leaning into him to avoid falling. I'm dizzy with desire and effort. I am the expatriate, the outsider, pried open by the visceral nature of this country, astounded by its impact on me, by the impact of this young man whom I always refer to in my mind, even as I hate myself for it, as The Chicken Fucker, offering me his arm, his shoulder, his body as support. The offer is kind, routine. The *manglar* stinks more in some places than others, a smell of rotting eggs. It's Easter, I want to forgive him, I want to tell him I know, it doesn't matter, I'm sure he paid and paid for fucking that chicken—Cortita had a passion for penance, she would have seen to that.

The mud clutches at my feet and legs. We're alongside the channel now, a deep wide muddy trough. On the other side mangrove roots dangle above the mud, in the air, dainty verticals waiting for the tide. Everything is base and beautiful here. Everything is just what it is. I will not tell Nicky any of this. I can't explain how it is that moments of love come at me from the craziest places, escaping from the gaseous pockets in the sucking mud, from the slippery strata of what we've seen and cannot avoid. This skin. This knowledge.

Orchids

I am sitting on a huge oil pipe by the side of the dirt road high in the mountains. It's as big as a conduit but I straddle it, not really waiting for cars or trucks, although you want me to flag them down. I don't know where you are right now, high in some tree out of sight, singling out a plant from a mass of orchids draped parasitic over the branch of one of these tall trees. I don't know where you are or how long you will take or if I will be able to drag you back to the road if you fall and hurt one of your two long legs. The day's crisp palette surrounds me, the green and gold of vegetation at this altitude, my jeans blue and bright against the dew-shine, dark rubber of the pipe. I am exceedingly happy not just because I love you—I do, in an innocent girl-next-door way, it's all I'm allowed, it's all I allow myself—but because I am free for these few precious moments without the obligation of destination, without the expectations you have of me that I am sadly not fulfilling. It was your idea, of course; it will be years before I know enough to take these moments for myself. You've dealt this hand today; you dealt it yesterday; you are growing tired of making all the decisions but we have not argued yet. That argument will come in a day or two in a town at a lower altitude and you will accuse and I will cry. Today your urge for orchids has lured you to strike a path through the verdant tangled growth.

You are somewhere out of sight, halfway up or down some slippery trunk and I am here and the day is perfect and I am daydreaming, I am an astronaut, I am a rider, I am a lovely lover: men flock to my side. I am writing a great book and painting many great paintings; I live on a horse ranch with a strange dark husband. I stride in and out of rooms wearing brown boots, and cream jodphurs, my white shirt open at the neck. I am hot, exhilarated and exhausted from my day's ride; guests await me, admiring. My dogs wheel and yelp around my legs. One word from me quiets them. I am the *patrona* and my servants bring me cool drinks in tall glasses on wide, dark wood trays.

And now you are coming back, happy, the small yellow flower on its stem bouncing from the top of your knapsack. Back in the city, a week from now, it will have been transplanted, hooked into a slice of corky root and hung just outside the door to the below-ground apartment we share. By then you'll have looked it up in the orchid book and told me its name, this tiny yellow perfection, another of the small wild parasites you are determined to raise as your own.

I thought I heard a car, you say. No, a *camioneta*, going the other way. But it is still morning and though you are now all timetable and urgency, I am clinging to my roadside reverie. We left Baesa in a spitting rain, after a breakfast of instant coffee and sweet bread. Last night we met the Peace Corps woman who made us tea on a tiny spirit stove and fed us damp biscuits and told us the local cows, most of them, are sick with a parasite. She trains the farmers to use imported medicines, to sterilize the knives they wield in the simple animal surgery that is practiced here. She is pretty and weary and has a thick gleaming braid of strawberry blond hair. Prolonged loneliness has made her distrust our imported friendliness, our city chatter. She warms a bit to you because everyone does. I do not know enough botany or biology to have a real conversation with her but you and she are talking plants. She says she is always cold here, has gotten used to it. Her Spanish, like yours, is fluent.

I ask her the name of the huge white flowers we saw earlier, sagging by the dozens from trees beside the river. Angel's Trumpet, she says. Oh. Not Belladonna? Close, she replies, same family. In Latin: *Solanaceae*, but you'd know it as Nightshade. She pauses. And both are poisonous.

You are frowning because I've interrupted. She sees our silent exchange, the volleying of looks across this player's net we carry everywhere we go. I know that she knows the score. When we leave her to eat our dinner in the only restaurant in town I am sad in a way I don't understand.

Dinner is dinner, they say when we ask. No choice. I know they think we're silly or *tonto*, stupid. Meat. Rice. Beans. Protein for the road. I am so thirsty and the choices are the ones we will encounter everywhere: the terrible coffee or the sick-sweet colas, pink and green. I whine a bit about it. You raise one eyebrow and give me that look, the one that says what-do-you-expect?

We sleep together every night, wound around each other for warmth because with sunset comes the bone-chilling cold. I know you resent this too at times, since mine is not the body you would choose to sleep beside or enter. This is another conversation we will have soon enough. When I ask and you will reply that you don't know how, it's been so long, women are now a foreign land. Shrugging your broad shoulders. You will say, "I am not the man you need," and show concern at how I've managed without it all this time. A small picture will grow in my mind of a domestic appliance, an Osterizer, dusty from disuse. Something needing service. This is how you see me. But we have not had these conversations yet, nor even found the small brook bubbling over mossed rocks where we will wash after the descent to view the famous waterfall; nor yet shivered under each other's naked gaze, our pinkening skin rinsed clear of dust and sweat, ourselves revealed in these true mountains.

In a little over a week's time I will faint in the coastal town, overcome with heat and the effects of malaria prophylactics, and then we will board a sturdy boat that will crash into a

larger ship enroute to another coastal town. For a few hollow
moments destiny will breathe its cool breath down our tense
necks and the world will stop and then we, with all the rest,
the too-many passengers on this boat without lifebuoys or
rafts, will move, en masse, a giant beetle with many legs and
arms, stretching, reaching, leaping, flowing in mid-ocean
from one boat to the tanker that is heading back in the direction from which we came until, only-in-Ecuador, the group
takes up a collection to bribe the new Capitan to change
course. We will get where we are going one half-day late, the
last to leave the tanker because we are gringos and neither
understand the etiquette nor have the confidence to jump
queue into the small overloaded *canoas* ferrying passengers to
shore for 200 sucres a head. News of us will have reached the
town where we are expected, news that *los rubios*, the blonds,
were on the boat that broke and will be coming. When? *Ya
mismo*, meaning: now, soon, someday, maybe, I don't know.

All of that is still to come, as is the hot town at the edge of the
jungle with cockroaches larger than I could have imagined
and a shit-smeared toilet too far down the hall and open-sided
buses and ragged running children, pointing, laughing, with
whom I play a kind of waving game that infuriates you, and
why is that? Because they stare more openly at me? We will
buy green metallic bugs and black velvety butterflies with
neon markings in the one real tourist town we hit during this
five-day circling tour of ours, the butterflies folded shut and
labelled in tiny triangles of waxed paper, the bugs rolled in
toilet paper and nailed into a balsa box. The owners of the store
will serve us something sweet and steeped and alcoholic and
show us how to inject water from a syringe into the dried
thorax of the butterfly to force it open for display, and they will
take us to the hot springs, these people who adopt us, these
people you always, always charm.

And still to come is a trip upriver by canoe to the house on stilts where the beautiful American artist lives with her trail-guide husband and their wild child son who pees like a dog because he has no human playmates, only this old and faithful German shepherd. While you are talking trails and botany with her Ecuadorian husband, she will show me pictures of her paintings, Bosch-like and disturbing, insisting that I read each title, discuss and respond to each image so that we will be tired and ready for bed before any mention is made of the fact that I too am a printmaker and painter. I am being conquered skillfully by this Belladonna, she is a pale heavy fruit hanging from a dark tree at the border of my dream when I finally fall to sleep after taking fright at the tarantulas in the outhouse. The next morning she will conquer you but it will be more mutual, her beauty firing hot and white against yours, and you will talk about orchids as if nothing else existed in the world. I will be ignored but not mind it too much, stunned by the a.m. beauty of the jungle, the morning glories big as saucers, beaming a blue so electric it hurts my heart. Her husband has found orchids no-one has documented before. Somehow she makes it sound as if this, too, is her accomplishment. When we leave their home, travelling again by canoe, I will not be sad to say goodbye, although I'll feel diminished and frumpy. Even you will look paler, bleached by her white hot need.

But none of this has come to pass because you are still out of sight, shimmying up or down some wet tree. And I cannot beckon that part of me to leave that roadside, to come down off that wide round oil pipe. I cannot take her into a future that is now my past, she will not budge or remove herself from reverie, from dreaming. She is whistling softly and smiling at the weeping gold and green surrounds, she is in gestation, waiting for a sign, a symbol, an orchid disentangled from its sybaritic perch, an orchid bouncing in its new found and temporary nest and everything she wants and needs, she has not learned yet. Because it's an art. Wanting. Needing. Knowing who you are.

It's only now, down the long tunnel of memory, that I see her innocence, perched and taking nourishment from air. You will be a part of a campaign, organized, it seems, to take that from her and so it is with the obstinacy of a child, with the grip of an orchid on its borrowed branch, that she is clinging to the time before the pain.